SMOKE BEFORE THE WIND

A NOVEL

SMOKE BEFORE THE WIND

DIANA WALLIS TAYLOR

Pleasant Word
A Division of WinePress Group

ISBN 13: 978-1-4141-1358-6
ISBN 10: 1-4141-1358-7
Library of Congress Catalog Card Number: 2008910262

CHAPTER ONE

CARRIE DICKSON BARELY listened to Professor Grant's last-minute instructions on his creative writing assignment due the following Friday, her mind already working on the story. She gathered her book backpack, and as she left the classroom, her friend Tori hurried up to her in the hall.

"Carrie! I'm so glad I caught you. Come with me to the Art of Espresso. Dean's waiting for me and he wants us to meet a friend of his."

"Tori, I have a class in half an hour. If this is another of your blind date ideas, skip it. I'm not interested."

"Look, Carrie, ever since Dave moved across the country to attend Columbia, you've been in a slump. He dumped you and it's time to move on. Don't let him have that kind of power over you. He's history."

"I will, in my own time. Seriously, I just don't want to date right now. Besides, Dave didn't dump me…we just agreed to part ways."

Tori rolled her eyes. "Right. So that's why you sat by the phone and haunted your mailbox?"

"Tori…"

"Okay. I'm sorry. I shouldn't have said it like that. I know it hurts, but you gotta let him go."

The breeze came up and Carrie brushed a wisp of blond hair back from her face. "I'm just not ready to meet anyone right now."

"Just because Dave was a jerk doesn't mean all guys are. In any case, I told Dean I'd bring you along. It'll just take a few minutes. At least say hello. Please?" The last word was stretched out along with a bright smile.

Carrie stopped and glared at her best friend. "Stop begging. All right. I'll give it ten minutes, and I'm gone. Okay?" She shook her head and began to walk briskly to keep up with Tori's pace.

"Dean's friend is Andrew Van Zant. Isn't that intriguing?"

"Sounds like he has a mustache and a goatee."

"Stop being negative. Besides being handsome, he's rich."

"You know that isn't the criteria I care about, Tori. Does he go to your church? How old is he anyway?"

"Whoa, girlfriend, I haven't seen him at church, and as for age, I don't know. Late twenties, I guess."

As they entered the café, they saw the two men at a table in the corner. They stood up as the women approached. Carrie had to admit that Andrew was attractive. He wore a tan, suede shirt that showed his broad shoulders—he was not only trim, but tall—at least six feet three.

Dean gave Tori a quick hug. "Hey, babe, glad you made it." He nodded to Carrie. "Nice to see you." He glanced at Tori and turned enthusiastically (too enthusiastically in Carrie's mind) toward his friend. "Carrie, this is Andrew Van Zant, a buddy of mine. Andrew, this is Carrie Dickson, a friend of Tori's."

Andrew reached out a hand and smiled at her. She looked up into a pair of twinkling brown eyes and a ruggedly handsome face. His smile revealed dimples on either side of his mouth, and his hair was tousled, giving him a boyish look.

Carrie took his hand briefly. "I'm glad to meet a friend of Dean and Tori's. Are you visiting in San Diego?"

He chuckled. "No, I live here, out in La Jolla."

The four of them sat down, and Dean jumped up again, to get them all coffee. Carrie started to object that she couldn't stay, but he was already ordering and she didn't want to make a scene. She'd be polite, but in a few minutes she was going to be out of there. *Thank goodness I have the excuse of another class to go to.*

Andrew was looking at her with obvious admiration, which was disconcerting. With a touch of irritation at feeling on display, she decided to ask some pointed questions. "How long ago did you graduate, Andrew?"

He seemed amused, and she wondered if he thought she was asking his age.

"I graduated eight years ago."

Tori chimed in. "Dean told me he used to edit the school newspaper right here at UCSD."

Carrie nodded. "So you went here. Are you in some form of journalism now?"

Dean returned and set the cardboard holder with four cups of coffee on the table and passed them out before he sat down.

Andrew stirred two packets of sugar into the steaming black liquid. "Actually I'm not. I work for my father in an antique, import business."

Tori leaned forward. "You should see some of those pieces, Carrie. Beautiful. I could go for a whole houseful." She grinned broadly at Andrew. "That is, if I could afford any."

Andrew gave her an appreciative smile and turned back to Carrie. "What's your field?"

"I'm going to be a teacher in the fall. I've signed a contract with the San Diego City School District."

He nodded approval. "A worthy occupation, teaching."

She shifted the subject back to him. "So how do you like the import business?"

"Well, it's a family business started by my grandfather 50 years ago. I hadn't planned on going that direction, but my grandfather died my senior year in college and my father convinced me he needed my help, so I didn't have much choice."

"I think each of us should choose our own field."

Andrew leaned back and his eyes held a trace of amusement. "I agree with you, Carrie Dickson. You wouldn't like to duke it out with my father, would you?"

She laughed and shook her head. "I don't think he would be interested in my opinion."

Dean slapped him on the shoulder. "That would be the day, buddy, when your dad asks anyone's opinion."

Tori leaned against Dean. "I'm so glad Dean decided to finish his last year here. We would never have met."

Dean grinned. "That's a bonus."

Carrie took a sip of her coffee. "How did you happen to transfer back here, Dean?"

"After I was discharged from the military, I got accepted to a college in the Midwest. But, my dad passed away last year and Mom was alone. Then she started having heart trouble. My sister and her family are in New York and couldn't make a change with their jobs and all. I didn't have any ties, so I came home to keep an eye on my mom."

Carrie smiled at him. "That was a nice thing to do, Dean. I'm sure your mom is glad to have you here."

Tori tucked her arm in Dean's. "He's going to be a high school physical education teacher. He'll make a great coach." She beamed at him.

Looking at Dean's muscular build, Carrie could easily picture him in a coaching job. She glanced at her watch and realized she had five minutes to make it to class. She'd have to finish her coffee on the run. As she stood up, both men rose also.

"It was nice meeting you, Andrew. I've got to go or I'll be late to my next class. Thanks for the coffee, Dean." He gave her a wave of his hand.

"I enjoyed meeting you too, Carrie..." Andrew began. She cut him off with a bright smile, said goodbye to Tori and Dean, and hurried away.

As soon as she was out of sight of the café, she tossed the coffee in the trash and half-walked, half-ran across the campus. As she neared the art building, she mused on the meeting. Andrew seemed nice enough, and he was good-looking, but she'd have so much going on to finish her last semester and graduate. She'd be driving home to Northern California to her family. Then, there were things she wanted to do during the summer before she tackled her first teaching job. She just didn't want to get involved with someone right now.

For a moment she allowed thoughts of Dave to cross her mind. Although they had never talked about it, most of their friends assumed they'd get married. They went to the same church off campus and had known each other for two years. Then Dave got the invitation from Colombia University for a special study program in his field, and he could talk of nothing else. She still remembered the last time they went out and how quiet he'd been when he walked her home. Instead of a romantic good night kiss, to her utter surprise, he took her hand, gave her a brotherly kiss on the cheek, and dropped a bombshell.

"Carrie, you know how much you mean to me, but things just aren't going to work out between us. I'll be three thousand miles away. I don't want any obstacles right now. I have my career to think of."

She'd looked at him, tears pooling in her eyes. "You see me as an obstacle?"

He shrugged. "It just isn't the right time. You're a great girl, Carrie. I wish you the best." Then, he turned and walked quickly away without a backward glance.

She'd stood there a long moment trying to comprehend what had just happened, and as the sobs rose in her throat, she hurried into her apartment before someone could see her and went to the rocking chair by the window. For a long time, she just sat there in the dark, letting the tears flow.

Now, as the scene faded in her mind, Carrie lifted her chin with determination. "I'm not interested. I don't care how handsome he is!" And she hurried into the art building.

When the phone rang that evening, she expected it to be Tori wanting to know her impression of Dean's friend.

The voice on the other end of the line was not Tori's.

"Hello, Carrie?"

"Yes?"

"Andrew Van Zant. We met today at the café."

Tori. You gave him my phone number. You're pushing the envelope, girlfriend!

"Yes?"

"I enjoyed meeting you. I was wondering if you'd let me take you to dinner one evening this week. I assure you I'm perfectly trustworthy."

She could imagine him grinning on the other end of the phone.

"I appreciate the invitation, Andrew, but I've got a project to complete for my creative writing class, and two tests coming up."

"I know a little Italian place in the Gas Lamp District. Do you like spaghetti?"

"Yes, but…"

"There's also a group that does folk dances in Balboa Park on Sundays. Have you ever seen them?"

Had Tori told him she'd done some folk dancing in high school? Just what else had Tori shared with him?

"No, I haven't."

"They're pretty good. I think you'd enjoy watching them. Why don't you let me pick you up after church on Sunday. After the folk dancing, we could have a simple dinner. What do you say?"

Carrie sighed. He was hard to resist. Tori must have told him that she went to church, but he didn't say anything about going himself. Andrew didn't strike her as the church-going type, but she'd soon find out.

He was waiting patiently for her answer. She rubbed the back of her neck with one hand. It had been seven months since Dave left. There couldn't be any harm in one Sunday dinner.

"That's nice of you, Andrew. I guess that would be all right."

"Wonderful. I'll pick you up Sunday afternoon."

They agreed on a time and she gave him directions to her apartment. After she hung up, she looked in the mirror. *So what do you think you're doing, Carrie? You don't know anything about this guy except he's a friend of Tori's boyfriend and he works in his father's import business.* She shook her head and picked up a legal pad to work on her story for class. After a while she laid the pad down. The creative muse had taken a break. She stared out the window and considered Andrew. In her mind's eye she saw a pair of warm brown eyes that crinkled when he smiled. But then, even though she tried not to think of it, the pain of Dave's broken promises hit her again.

Chapter Two

ANDREW ARRIVED PROMPTLY and didn't ask to come in, which pleased her. She grabbed her sweater and locked the door.

He opened the car door for her and as she slid into the beige leather, cushioned upholstery—she felt like she was in an arm chair. It was a convertible but he'd put the top up. She hadn't noticed the make of the car, but it was black, low slung, and reeked of expensive. Obviously the import business was doing well.

He made light conversation as they drove into Balboa Park and found a parking place. As they approached a large ornate building, Carrie could hear Greek music. She recognized the steps to the Greek Kolo as she watched. The dancers wove around the room in a line led by a young man in black pants, black boots, and an embroidered, white shirt. He was waving a white kerchief. The group then did a Lithuanian dance and a more complicated dance called the Russian Peasant.

Carrie was not aware of the delighted look on her face until she turned to Andrew to tell him about one of the dances and saw he was watching her, an amused smile on his face. Her cheeks got red. "I always did enjoy the different steps to the dances. They're sometimes pretty intricate. The Russian Peasant has around nineteen steps to the dance." She stopped suddenly—aware she was rambling.

"I'm glad you're enjoying it."

They stayed over an hour until the folkdance group took a break and, then, they drove downtown to the Gas Lamp District.

The restaurant was a small, hole-in-the-wall place, but crisp white tablecloths draped every table, and it was cozy.

"*Signore* Van Zant! *Buenvenito!*" The proprietor, Gino, gave Carrie the eye and, wiggling his heavy eyebrows, grinned broadly. Evidently she'd passed the test. He seated them with a flourish.

"Wait until you taste his spaghetti sauce, Carrie. It's outstanding."

While they waited for the spaghetti, Gino brought a bottle of red wine and held it out for Andrew's approval. He nodded and Gino poured some in his glass. Andrew tasted it and grinned. Gino turned to pour some in Carrie's glass, but she quickly put her hand over the glass.

"None for me, but thank you."

Gino frowned, raised his eyebrows at Andrew, and shrugged with his palms up. He went to get their dinners.

Andrew studied her, thoughtfully. "You don't drink wine, Carrie?"

She gave a small shrug. "No."

"Any particular reason? Lots of church-going people drink wine."

She sighed. "The church I grew up in believed in avoiding liquor. I've just never wanted any."

He leaned back, looking a little smug. "You know, of course, that they made beer back in Biblical times and drank wine."

It was her turn to raise her eyebrows. "How did you know that?"

"An avid reader, eclectic you might say."

She didn't know how to respond and remained silent.

He leaned forward and put his elbows on the table. "So, tell me about yourself, Carrie."

Andrew sipped his wine and asked casual questions as they ate. He found out her mother ran a bookshop and coffeehouse in their community and her father worked for the Forestry Department. He was such an attentive listener that she found herself telling him more than usual about herself, including her frustrating relationship with her cousin, Linda, who'd always out-staged her in high school.

"Linda's parents were killed in a small plane crash when she was ten and she came to live with us. It's when she got old enough to notice boys the trouble began."

He coiled some spaghetti neatly on his fork. "And what trouble was that?"

"She was boy crazy. Every time I liked someone, she found a way to steal him away. She's like a magnet for guys."

He pause, fork in mid-air, and looked her in the eyes. "Apparently they just didn't know a good thing when they saw it."

Carrie blushed. His gaze was a little too direct.

When at last he walked her to her door of her apartment, she again braced herself for the usual request to come in. It wasn't forthcoming. Instead he took her hand.

"Thanks for a nice evening, Carrie. I'd like to call you again. May I?"

Would he? She merely answered, "That would be nice, Andrew."

As she watched him drive away, her mind was bombarded with thoughts. On one hand, she wanted to see him again, and on the other hand, she was pretty sure he wasn't a Christian. He had good manners and hadn't forced himself on her—that was to his credit. Should she see him again? Shaking the thoughts away, she closed the door and slid the bolt in place.

To her surprise, Andrew managed to see her as often as he could get away from the store and he proved extremely creative in planning things to do. They shared popcorn at the movies, went to an auto demolition derby, and took in a couple of documentary films at the IMAX in the park.

His tastes were eclectic and she never knew whether he would call her with tickets to a ball game or the opera. She'd haunted her favorite discount store for some dressy outfits, but dating Andrew was putting a big dent in her clothing budget. For their evening at the opera, she'd found a cranberry velveteen dress with a matching jacket. Andrew wore a tux, and she was glad she'd gone to the extra trouble with her makeup and accessories because he introduced her to more people than she could possibly remember in the lobby. His social world was exciting, but challenging.

Although he knew she was a Christian, he never talked about his own spiritual convictions. Carrie knew it would mean heartache if she got attached to someone who didn't share her faith, but the time hadn't seemed right for a deep discussion. Besides, she was having such a wonderful time and part of her didn't want to risk ending that.

One day when Andrew called he asked, "Do you like trains?"

"Yes, but I've only ridden on one a couple of times."

"Good, I'll pick you up Sunday afternoon at one o'clock."

She laughed in exasperation as she listened to the dial tone. He didn't ask her if she had other plans.

Sunday afternoon, as they turned into Balboa Park, Carrie was puzzled. There were no trains in the park except the kiddie ride. Then, as they walked, she realized where they were going.

"You were talking about miniature trains, Andrew. Why didn't you tell me?"

He grinned. "I thought you might think it was boring. Besides, these are really something. All the men who did the landscaping and laid the tracks are volunteers."

She smiled at his eagerness. *Big boys who still love to play with trains.*

They spent over an hour watching the dozen or so trains run through mountains and miniature villages. Andrew asked the volunteers quite a few questions.

It was almost three o'clock when they wandered down the Prado to get a sandwich and some hot chocolate. March had arrived with its cold weather and gusty breezes.

As they started back to the car, it began to rain and, laughing, they pulled their coats over their heads and ran.

When they got in the car, Andrew took her chin in his hand and she realized he was going to kiss her. Her heart was pounding, but reason asserted itself. She wasn't ready for that. She gently removed his hand and sat back.

There was a shadow in Andrew's dark eyes, but he only looked thoughtful and turned to start the car.

Carrie struggled to rein in her emotions. She was attracted to Andrew, and she knew it.

She finally asked, "Andrew, would you go to church with me this Sunday?"

He shut off the motor and turned to her. She wasn't sure it was annoyance or that he was contemplating her request.

"How about coming to my church next Sunday?" he responded.

Her eyes widened. 'Your church? You've never mentioned it."

He waved a hand casually. "I don't go that often, but church seems important to you. I thought you might like to go. I hear there is a guest speaker."

"All right. What time is the service?"

"Eleven. I'll pick you up about ten fifteen."

He started the car and drove her home. Neither one spoke much on the entire drive. *This would be the perfect time to ask about his faith,* Carrie thought, but somehow, silence felt more comfortable.

CHAPTER THREE

*T*HE STONE BLOCKS of the church looked like they had been there for a hundred years. Andrew looked handsome in a tan suit with a beige and blue tie. As they entered the church, he led Carrie to a pew about five rows from the front. When they sat down, she noted a small, gold name plate on the pew that said it was donated by Jacob Van Zant. *His grandfather?* She glanced at the name plate and raised her eyebrows at Andrew but he didn't comment. *What was this morning about?*

They sang "A Mighty Fortress Is Our God," repeated their Scripture responses from the program led by a deacon, and listened as the choir sang an offertory. There was one more hymn and then the sermon. The pastor was eloquent as he spoke of their role as Christians in society, but there was no mention of the Gospel or an invitation to make Christ part of one's life. Used to the praise hymns and more informal service at home, it seemed very solemn to Carrie, yet she pictured herself standing by Andrew's side every Sunday and let her imagination run amok.

As they strolled back to Andrew's car, he turned toward her. "What did you think of the service?"

"It was very…nice, Andrew. Very, ah…"

"Dull?"

"I didn't think it was dull, Andrew. It was just different from what I'm used to."

"In what way?"

She shrugged. "Well, we have different music—choruses as well as hymns, and instead of an organ accompaniment, we have several guitars, and drums."

He turned suddenly to stare at her. "Drums? In a church?"

"He plays them softly. It just all kind of goes together." She cocked her head to one side. "Maybe sometime you'd like to try my church."

He stuck his hands in his pockets. "I never had much time for church. My father only went on special occasions. I think it's called keeping up appearances."

She noted the sarcastic tone of his voice and decided to drop the subject, for now.

He loosened his tie. "How about a drive up the coast? I know a restaurant that has some great seafood."

They drove to Cardiff and had lunch at a restaurant that had big windows where they could look out at the ocean. Afterward, on impulse, Andrew took off his jacket, shoes, and socks, and rolled up his pant legs. Carrie went into the ladies room and took off her stockings. The day was sunny, but cool, as hand in hand they strolled on the beach. Andrew dug up a sand crab, putting it in her hand. Then, he looked down at her with her hair blowing in the breeze. He put a hand on the back of her neck and drew her to him for a kiss. This time, in spite of herself, she responded.

"Why don't we go back to your place," he whispered huskily, and kissed her again.

The reality of what he was asking was clear, and it took all of her will power to step away and look him full in the face. "I think you need to take me home, Andrew, but not come in."

"Right." A trace of irritation crossed his face, but he covered it. They turned back and Andrew walked so swiftly she had trouble keeping up with him.

Without a word, he drove her home, escorted her to the door of her apartment, and then turned and walked away. Carrie flung herself on her bed and wept.

Two days later, he sent flowers and called to apologize.

The wind blew small gusts of rain as they sat in his car on a bluff overlooking the sea at Ocean Beach. They munched on chicken sandwiches Andrew had picked up at a nearby deli.

He seemed in a thoughtful mood as he stared out at the blue-green water before them watching the few hardy souls that jogged by. Others hurried along the path at the top of the cliffs hunched into their jackets as they walked their dogs.

"Do you like antiques?" He asked suddenly.

She lowered her sandwich and glanced at him. "Yes, I think so. My parent's home has a little of everything. My mom loves interesting furniture."

"Sounds like my kind of person." Then he clammed up again.

Thinking back on their first conversation in the café, she sought some sort of conversational opening. "You said your father needed you in the import business, but that isn't what you want to do."

He shrugged. "No. I was interested in being a journalist, traveling around the world, picking up interesting stories. But my dad wouldn't hear of it. It's as if I told him I want to be a drug smuggler or something."

"Doesn't he want you to do what you want to do?"

"Not really. When my grandfather died, he took over the business and built it up to what it is today—for me, he says. The fact that I don't want to be in the import business seems, I guess, disloyal from his viewpoint."

"That must be hard to live with. What are you going to do?"

He took another bite of his sandwich and chewed thoughtfully a moment.

"Well, for now, I guess I'll stick to the import business. It's doing well, and I found I enjoy bidding on estates. Fortunately, it involves some traveling."

Silence prevailed again as they watched the waves crash one after another on the rocks below. The ocean seemed to almost caress the pools and crevasses with foamy fingers before sliding back into the dark green water. The sky was rapidly turning gray as the wind came up churning the brooding water into whitecaps.

Carrie was tempted to ask when she would get to meet Dietrich Van Zant, but Andrew didn't offer and she didn't want to seem presumptive. Sensing the animosity that existed between father and son, she knew if Andrew wanted her to meet his father, he'd suggest it in his own time.

He had one arm along the back of the seat and with his other hand he suddenly reached over and drew a finger along her cheek. With a question in his eyes, he brought the arm down around her shoulders and gently pulled her toward him. Once again when he kissed her, she responded. He kissed her again and then leaned back studying her face pensively—as if he needed to make up his mind about something.

Later, when Andrew had dropped her off at home, she put her purse down and walked over to the window. Andrew puzzled her. Did he really care for her, or was she just one of a string of young women who passed through his life? He was warm and attentive, but sometimes distracted. She shook her head. Perhaps it was just the situation with his father that occupied his mind.

CHAPTER FOUR

*M*ID-TERMS WERE over and March slid into April. Andrew took her to concerts, movies, and out for hamburgers and fries. One day they went to the park and watched a kite club fly their fragile creations that dipped and soared in the April breeze.

He sent her a text message to meet him at the café the next day, and after lunch with little or no conversation, they strolled across campus as he walked her to the science building. *Now what is bothering him?* Carrie wondered. They came to the back of the building, and he suddenly pulled her into the shadows under a tree where he kissed her roughly, almost harshly. She caught her breath and looked up at him with questions in her eyes. *Andrew?* Her heart was beating erratically in her chest. She was in love with him but why did she have the feeling he was holding her at arm's length emotionally? These brooding moods came and went, leaving her alternately confused and determined to mend whatever was bothering him.

He looked out at the campus and then turned back to her. "Would you like to meet my father?"

At last, but why is he asking now? He hadn't invited her in all these months. Somehow she sensed it wasn't a time for questions. She gave him a bright smile. "Why, I'd love to meet your father, Andrew."

He had a cup of coffee while she finished her class; then, they drove to La Jolla. He pulled into the parking lot of an enormous building with etched glass double doors. They passed through several rooms of elegant furniture in warm and dark polished woods and silk fabrics. Carrie paused to look at an ornate armoire. The price was twelve thousand dollars. She quickly continued walking behind Andrew.

As they entered an office, a young woman was working on a computer. Her desk appeared to be an orderly jumble of paperwork. She was pretty in a very sophisticated way, and the red hair curving around her face accented a peaches and cream complexion.

She looked up as Andrew approached and Carrie saw a fleeting glimpse of excitement in the girl's green eyes before she hid it behind a professional attitude.

Andrew perched on the edge of her desk and turning to Carrie, waved in the girl's direction.

"Carrie, this is Jana Carroll, my father's right hand lady. She juggles clients, handles the books, and is just amazing. Jana, this is Carrie Dickson. I'm showing her around today. Is my father in? I thought Carrie would like to meet him."

Jana gave Carrie a brief once over, masked by a polite smile. The question in her eyes, and her hand on Andrew's arm, made Carrie a little uncomfortable. Had she been an item with Andrew at one time? Was she now?

"Actually, he wants to see you, alone."

Carrie didn't miss the emphasis on the last word. She waved a hand. "You go ahead, I'll just wander around the store."

Andrew ran his fingers through his hair, straightened his shoulders, and winked at Jana.

"If I'm not out in twenty minutes, send in the paramedics."

Jana laughed charmingly and watched him as he entered his father's office and closed the door behind him.

Though the walls somewhat muffled the sound, the argument taking place in the other room had the two women's full attention. Carrie stood and listened with growing alarm. Mr. Van Zant was obviously furious with Andrew over something.

Without warning the door jerked open and Andrew stalked out. He had a grim set to his mouth. He glanced at Jana for a moment and then took Carrie's elbow. As they were about to leave, a large man appeared behind them in the doorway, his expression dark and angry. He observed Carrie and raised his eyebrows slightly.

"You didn't mention bringing a guest. Were you planning on introducing me?"

Seeing Carrie's obvious discomfort, Andrew paused, and with a theatrical wave said, "Carrie, this is the Lord of the import business, my father, Dietrich Van Zant. This is a friend, Carrie Dickson."

Dietrich Van Zant flashed a warning glance at his son, and started to say something, but apparently thought better of it. He turned to Carrie with a tight smile.

"A pleasure, my dear. Do come in." He stepped aside and indicated the open doorway.

Andrew muttered an expletive under his breath and reluctantly followed Carrie into the room he'd left in anger only moments before.

The large walnut paneled office was a study in elegance with soft blue and cinnamon woven draperies. Several oil paintings adorned the walls. Most were nature scenes and the one behind his desk was a beautiful seascape with waves smashing against rocks. She could almost feel the spray in her face. The force of the painting seemed to mirror that of the man before her, dominating the room.

She faced Andrew's father across a desk of deep cherry wood the size of a dining room table. Shifting carefully from one foot to another, she felt as if she was being swallowed up by the plush carpeting. Was she to stand or sit?

"Do sit down, Ms. Dickson."

She sat, but Andrew remained standing, leaning against the doorway with his arms folded across his chest, his face the picture of offended pride.

Dietrich Van Zant must be at least six feet four, Carrie thought as he towered above her. His gray hair, mostly white at the temples, framed a strong, square face. It was easy to see where his son had gotten his build and rugged good looks.

For a man who appeared used to giving orders, he surprised Carrie by sitting down, his face tired and thoughtful.

"You met at the University?"

"Yes, through some mutual friends." *Hadn't Andrew told his father anything about their relationship?*

"And you're going to be a teacher." *Then, they had talked about her.*

"Yes, I'll be teaching second grade in September."

"Ah, someone with a millennium of patience."

He put the tips of his fingers together. "Where's your home, my dear? Tell me about yourself."

She hesitated, but with a quick glance at Andrew, plunged in. "I'm from a small town in northern California. My father works for the forest service and my mother runs a small bookshop and coffeehouse in the historic district." She stopped suddenly, not sure how much he wanted to know.

Mr. Van Zant was silent a long moment, and she studied her hands in her lap, finding it difficult to face those piercing eyes.

When she finally looked up, she found him contemplating her over the small teepee he made of his fingers.

This time Carrie met his eyes.

He stood up suddenly. "You've chosen an excellent field, Ms. Dickson. I wish you every success. Do come and see me, again, sometime." *End of brief interrogation.*

"Thank you, sir, I'd like that."

He escorted her to the door preceded by Andrew and shook her hand, then returned to his office and closed the door firmly.

Andrew nearly dragged her out of the building, and she imagined she could feel the eyes of Jana Carroll boring into her back.

Well, she'd met the infamous Dietrich Van Zant. Andrew was into one of his blue funks and seemed preoccupied. He dropped her off at her apartment and gave her an absentminded kiss.

"I'll call you, okay?"

Her voice seemed small in her ears. "Okay." *Was he going to be another Dave?*

Later that week, Carrie was soaking in her claw-footed tub, immersed in gardenia bubble bath. Her head felt clogged with information. Studying for finals had made her brain tired. Squeezing the soapy sponge over her shoulders, she contemplated her relationship with Andrew. He hadn't called for several days. *Was it over?* Thoughts of Andrew made studying difficult. She felt she was more interested in him than he was in her. A wave of apprehension struck. Where was their relationship headed? She'd skipped church several times to do things with him and most of the time he was such fun to be with that she rationalized her guilt. After all, he did promise to come to church with her one Sunday, soon.

She glanced at the phone and frowned. If willing it to ring had worked, it would have rung a hundred times over.

She slipped into her nightgown and robe and wandered into the closet-sized kitchen to stare at her pantry cupboard. *What was that nursery rhyme about Old Mother Hubbard?* She made a mental note to write out a grocery list and settled for a can of minestrone soup. There was a small piece of cheese and three slices of bread left, including two heels. Oh well, half a cheese sandwich would go with the soup. She wrinkled her nose. Creative cooking for one had lost its attraction after the first few months alone in her apartment.

As she curled up on the sofa, she picked up a textbook to read three chapters for one of her classes. The beat of the music in the next apartment pounded in her brain. *Eight thirty.* Cut-off time for noise was ten o'clock, an hour and a half away. She abandoned the idea of reading and went to wash up her few dishes.

The phone rang startling her and she raced to answer it.

"Carrie?"

"Andrew?" She sighed with relief and her heart began a steady rock beat in her chest.

"I had to be out of town on some business. An estate sale. Have you had dinner yet?"

You could have called, even from out of town. She glanced at the empty soup bowl. "Yes, I have."

"Ah, okay. I was hoping to take you out to dinner."

"Andrew, it's after eight thirty."

"Sorry. I didn't check the time. How about tomorrow night, unless you've made other plans?"

His words sounded a little fuzzy. Perhaps it was the phone connection.

"Well, I hadn't made any plans, yet."

"Great! I'll pick you up at seven thirty. Dress up my girl, we'll do the town."

There was a click and Carrie sat with the phone in her hand. A voice in the back of her head told her she was walking on dangerous ground. She ignored it.

CHAPTER FIVE

CARRIE BRUSHED HER hair until the blond highlights shone and turned from one side to the other, pleased with the way the cornflower blue, silk dress flowed from her slender waist. The dress was almost the color of her eyes. It was a splurge out of her tight budget, but she wanted to look especially nice. When she heard Andrew's special knock, she took a deep breath and hurried to open the door.

He stood with his hands in his pockets, leaning back on his heels. He wore an obviously well-pressed dark suit with a white silk turtleneck. He stepped back and looked her over from top to bottom, letting out a low whistle.

"You're gorgeous."

Something was different about him this time, but she wasn't sure what it was. He seemed a little uneasy, which was unusual.

He waited expectantly. He'd never been inside her apartment. It was an unspoken agreement. She hesitated and finally stood aside.

"Would you like to come in?"

He raised his eyebrows and stepped inside. His eyes were bright as he surveyed the room. The small white hide-a-bed couch she'd bought at a second hand shop, decorated with colorful throw pillows had a patchwork quilt folded over the back. She'd found the old rocking chair at a yard sale. It sat on an oval braided rug in blues and greens which covered the worn spot on the beige carpet. She followed his eyes over to the windowsill where a variety of plants, including a bright red geranium, spilled over in various odd containers.

"Would you like a cup of coffee…or…something?" What was it about Andrew being in her small place tonight that made her uncomfortable?

This was a different Andrew. His manner tonight was not casual.

"I would prefer a…something. What do you have?"

"Well, I have orange juice, tea, and um…some root beer."

"Root beer?" He wheeled around and studied her for a moment. "I think it's about time I educate you in the fine art of beverages, Carrie.'

She gave him a puzzled glance.

He shook his head. "Never mind, why don't we just get going?"

He took her arm and guided her toward the door.

Carrie began to wonder about the coming evening. Instead of his Porsche, a taxi waited at the curb. At her questioning glance, he murmured, "Parking is terrible downtown. This is easier."

The driver stopped in front of a tall building. As they passed through gold etched glass doors and took an elevator to the top floor, Carrie realized with a start that they were entering La Rouge, one of the most expensive restaurants in town. She had read about it in the newspaper's restaurant review section.

The maitre'd showed them to a table by the window, and Carrie gazed out at a spectacular view of the city. Menus were produced with a flourish, but as she opened hers she soon noted everything was a la carte and her thrifty soul gasped inwardly at the prices.

The waiter appeared and smiled in a deferential manner. "Will you have a cocktail while you are waiting, sir?"

Andrew glanced at Carrie and then shook his head. "Ah, I'll pass on that." He ordered a bottle of wine that she couldn't pronounce.

"Very good, sir." He took himself away and returned with the wine. Andrew sniffed the small amount in the glass, tasted it, and nodded in approval.

The waiter filled his glass and turned to fill her wine glass.

"No, thank you."

"Yes, madam." He picked up her wine glass and bore it off.

Andrew moved the dark red liquid around in the glass. "You really ought to try this, Carrie, it's delicious."

She gave him a reproving glance. "You know how I feel, Andrew."

Andrew was regarding her with amusement. "Not even on special occasions?"

She shrugged self-consciously, "No," and then her eyes widened. "Is this a special occasion?"

He smiled benevolently and murmured, "We'll see."

When he looked at her the way he was at this moment, her heart lurched within her. She gathered her wobbly feelings under control.

The halibut with a special cream sauce was delicious, and so tender it almost fell apart under her fork.

She concentrated on enjoying her dinner as Andrew tackled a steak, sipped his wine, and asked casual questions. At this moment he was his usual, charming self, entertaining her with stories of various clients who had come in the store. They laughed together over the woman who wanted her prize poodle to choose the couch for her living room.

He listened attentively as she described her last writing assignment and the problem with the plumbing in her apartment.

The waiter whisked their plates from the table and turned to Andrew.

"Shall I bring the dessert cart for your perusal, sir?"

"Would you like something, Carrie?"

"Oh, I'm not sure I can…well, maybe something light?" She looked hopefully at the waiter.

"May I suggest for madam, the crème brûlée? A light custard with a touch of lemon and a flame-hardened crust of brown sugar and ground macadamia nuts."

Crème brûlée was her favorite dessert, and when it came she savored every bite.

Andrew ordered coffee for both of them and as they waited, he reached across the table and took her hand.

"Carrie, how do you feel about love at first sight? Do you think it's possible?"

She caught her breath and slowly nodded her head.

He paused, choosing his words. "I think when two people meet and find they're in love, they should do something about it. Don't you?"

She nodded again but butterflies took flight in her stomach.

"Carrie, you take my breath away every time I see you. I think about you during the day, and at night I see you in my dreams. I've come to a realization that life without you isn't going to be worth anything."

He rubbed his thumb against her hand and her heart began to beat erratically in her chest. Was he leading up to what she thought he was leading up to?

He reached in his pocket, pulled out a small box and handed it to her. With trembling fingers she opened it to find a beautiful star fire diamond with baguettes surrounding it.

"Will you marry me, Carrie?"

Overcome by emotion, she found herself nodding her head again, her eyes pooling with tears. Her Cinderella dreams were coming true.

He took the ring out of the box and slipped it on her ring finger. "It was my grandmother's. I kept it after my mother died, just for that special girl I knew would come along one day. I know she would have been happy for us."

She couldn't take her eyes off the ring as it sparkled in the candlelight. She became aware of the murmur of voices at nearby tables. People gave them indulgent smiles and there was a round of applause, which Andrew acknowledged with a wide smile and a nod of his head. Carrie glanced around self-consciously.

When they at last rose from the table, Andrew smiled down at her. "That was a great dinner."

When he put his arm around her shoulders, for a moment she wasn't sure if he was guiding her or holding on.

The same taxi was miraculously waiting for them. Andrew nodded to the driver. "His name is Al. He's a gardener by day and tells me he drives a taxi on weekends to help support his family."

Carrie beamed at him and displayed her ring.

Al congratulated them, and Andrew took her in his arms and kissed her soundly as Al whisked them off to the Plaza Room. When her head cleared from Andrew's kiss, she noted the cost of "standing time" by Al's meter. This evening was costing Andrew a fortune!

An orchestra was playing as they entered the lounge, and once more, they got preferred treatment. He led her to the dance floor and they began to move to the music. She'd always loved to dance and followed him step for step. Dreamily she imagined they were Fred Astaire and Ginger Rogers. As the tempo slowed, he held her against him and she breathed the scent of his aftershave lotion.

When they finally sat down, she fanned herself with her hand. "It's so warm in here." She knew it was more than the exertion of the dance.

Andrew looked at her with that slight smile. "Yes, I noticed."

This kind of evening took a lot of one's energy. To her acute embarrassment her eyes seemed to have a will of their own. She massaged the back of her neck, trying not to make it obvious.

"Would you like to dance again?" She wondered where he got all his energy.

"Oh, it would be lovely, but do you mind if we sit this one out?" She slipped off her shoes under the table and rubbed one foot against the other. She needed to go home.

To her immense relief, Andrew looked at his watch. "Looks like we need to leave or they're going to close the place down on us."

Carrie looked around and realized that they were the last couple there. The band was putting away their instruments and the waiter stood to one side with a polite smile pasted on his face. She quickly slipped her shoes back on and stood up.

Al had been dozing in the taxi and straightened up when Andrew knocked on the window. He remembered where Carrie lived without having the directions repeated. Andrew leaned in the window of the taxi and spoke to Al briefly, and then walked her to her door. Had Andrew asked him to wait? Andrew took her key and opened her door. It was the moment of truth. They'd had a wonderful evening and they were engaged. She suddenly felt panicky. He was too near and her heart was knocking in her chest. Pretending to yawn, she looked up at him apprehensively.

"The ring is beautiful, Andrew. I'm still a little overcome."

He chuckled, tipped her chin up, and when he kissed her she swayed toward him. Fighting for control of her emotions, she stepped back only to find herself against the wall. Andrew touched her stricken face with his hand.

"Darling, you don't have to worry. I'm going home. One of the things I love about you is that you are a sweet girl." He smiled down at her as she stood in his arms. "I plan on taking good care of you. You're my future."

Still recovering from the kiss, she could only give him a lopsided smile.

He gently pushed her inside. "I'll call you, tomorrow, okay?"

She nodded wordlessly.

With a wink, he strolled back to the taxi.

CHAPTER SIX

*F*ROM THE TIME Andrew took her to share their good news with his father, everything seemed to be on fast forward. Jana smiled brightly and admired the engagement ring, but her eyes told a different story. Carrie saw the pain.

Dietrich Van Zant was extraordinarily pleased with the engagement, but there appeared to still be some tension between father and son.

"We need to set a date for the wedding, my dear. What would you say to the Fourth of July?"

Carrie gasped. "But that's only about eight weeks away. I still have graduation ceremonies."

"Then don't you worry your pretty head. I'll just take care of all the arrangements."

"But, Mr. Van Zant, I haven't even introduced Andrew to my family yet. I need a little more time."

Andrew stepped forward. "Darling, I turn 30 at the end of July. I promised myself I'd be married before then." He glanced at his father. "I'd hate to pass up that date."

She looked from one smiling face to the other. "Well, I guess Andrew could meet my parents at graduation. They'll be there."

Andrew shrugged apologetically. "I'm afraid I'm going to have to miss that occasion." He looked at his father steadily. "You wanted me to appraise the Medina collection?"

Dietrich Van Zant shot his son a strange look and placed a fatherly arm around Carrie's shoulders. "Perhaps Andrew could come up for a weekend and meet your family as soon as he gets back."

There was a hollow feeling at the pit of her stomach. This was not going the way she dreamed it would when she got engaged.

"I suppose that would be better. Perhaps we could have an open house and our friends and neighbors could meet Andrew."

"Yes, my dear. That's a wonderful idea." Dietrich turned to his son. "You could manage that, couldn't you, Andrew?"

As if on cue, Andrew nodded his head. "It would be a pleasure. Carrie and I will discuss that and work it out."

With his arm still around Carrie's shoulders, she felt Andrew's father propelling her toward the door.

Puzzled, Carrie turned to him. "Would you like to go over some things I've been thinking about for the wedding? Andrew and I could be married in our Community Church. I've gone there all my life. I'm sure the pastor will want to meet Andrew and talk with us."

There was a profound silence.

"I'm sure that is a wonderful idea, my dear, but I suggest the wedding take place at our church. We've had an engraved pew there for nearly 50 years. It would be easier for the caterers and there are a great number of important people we will be inviting."

Carrie's chest tightened. "I suppose that's all right."

Andrew took her arm. "We'll talk about it, darling. We need to go."

She let him lead her out of the building, but she didn't feel like talking.

As he handed her into the car, Andrew kissed her on the cheek. "Don't mind my father, Carrie, he means well. I'm his only son and he wants to make sure things are done right."

She felt their first quarrel coming on. "Do you think I'm incapable of planning my own wedding? I've looked forward to this day all my life, Andrew."

Her eyes flashed and before he could reply, she waved a hand at him. "I'm also an only child and my family will want to be part of this, too."

He went around the car and slid into the driver's seat. "I do understand, darling. Tell you what. When I come up we'll discuss the whole thing with your folks, okay? Now how about that beautiful smile?"

Somewhat mollified, she gave him a watery smile. "All right."

That evening she took a deep breath and picked up the phone to call her parents.

"Mom, get Dad on the other line. I have something to tell you." She broke the news and after getting over her shock, Helen murmured that the name sounded aristocratic, like an Old World duchess, but then her mother liked interesting names, working with books all the time.

Her father was more reserved. "We'll look forward to meeting this young man, cricket, just as soon as you can get him up here. Are you sure he can't make your graduation?"

"No, Daddy, he has to go out of town for his father. He'll come up in two weeks."

"Well, all right. We'll see you at your graduation ceremonies."

"I can't wait. I love you, Mom, Dad."

She rang off and wondered if she should prepare Andrew for the grilling he was sure to get from her father.

Ignoring the small voice in her head that whispered caution, she allowed her thoughts to be immersed in wedding dreams.

Graduation came and went in a whirl. Her parents flew from San Francisco, catching a commuter flight there from Redding. Linda sent regrets as her boss had come down with the flu. Someone else was missing her big day but Carrie put on a bright face and resolved to be matter of fact about it. She wouldn't let her folks know how disappointed she was that Andrew wasn't there. She couldn't even show them the ring as it was being sized and she couldn't pick it up until two days after graduation. She had an orchid corsage from Andrew and his father but having frequently checked her messages, there was no word from her fiancé.

The next day, with the graduate breakfast, getting to the college and talking with old friends, getting ready for the ceremonies, there was no time to talk about Andrew. She was relieved, but knew her dad was biding his time.

As she finally walked across the stage, elated that her years of college over, and received her diploma, her folks applauded loudly. She posed for what seemed like a hundred pictures, hugged her friends with tears of goodbye and promises to keep in touch, and turned in her gown. They drove to Old Town for Mexican food which they all loved, and too soon it was time to drive her folks back to the airport. Fire season was coming around and Mike needed to get back.

With a promise she'd be along in a few days when she got her apartment settled, she waved them off. There was still no word from Andrew and finally, fighting tears, she occupied herself with packing some of her things.

CHAPTER SEVEN

*T*HREE DAYS AFTER graduation, Carrie was on her way home. Her Mustang convertible hummed along the freeway as she drove north, each mile bringing her closer to her destination.

She'd been driving eight hours, checking in with her mom frequently.

She'd called Andrew several times but got his answering service each time. She frowned at the phone. Maybe he was in an area where the reception wasn't good. Feeling out of sorts, Carrie put her phone on the seat and prepared to enter traffic again. Her phone rang and, hoping it was Andrew, she snatched it up. It was her mother. She evidently picked up on the petulant tone in Carrie's voice.

"Darling, you must be tired after these last couple of weeks. It's almost six o'clock. You know we want you to be home as soon as possible, but I think I would rest easier if you stopped now and found a nice motel to spend the night."

"Mom, I have a convertible and it's packed. I can't leave it in the parking lot of a motel. It would be too easy to break into."

There was a pause. "I've got an idea. Stay where you are and I'll call you right back."

Carrie bought a coke from the vending machine and walked around a little, stretching her legs. After about ten minutes her phone rang again.

"Darling, I called a friend of mine who lives in Sacramento. She is a widow and enjoys having company. She would love to have you stay overnight, and she lives in a gated mobile home park so your things would be safe."

When her mother made up her mind, Carrie knew it was useless to argue. She took down the directions and promised to call when she got there.

She clicked her phone shut and pulled out of the rest stop. Twenty-five minutes later she drove into the gated community. Her name had been left with the guard and after a few turns on various streets, she pulled up to a lovely mobile home with roses in the yard. A rabbit was nibbling on one of the small plants. Carrie was delighted and sat watching for a moment.

A woman came out to meet her. She looked to be in her seventies and was wearing a pair of navy blue slacks and a blue and white top. She had a gentle face and short curly white hair. She was smiling as she approached the car.

"Carrie? I'm Norma Dillard. Your mother called me. I'm so glad to be able to help you. That's such a long drive." She gave Carrie a brief hug of welcome.

"It is so nice of you to take me in."

"Well, your mother was right. You should not be staying at a motel by yourself."

She turned toward the house. "I'm sure you're exhausted, dear. You just come on in and make yourself at home."

The mobile home was more like a modular home and furnished elegantly. Norma led her to a large bedroom that had soft pink drapes and a quilted rose bedspread. It was lovely.

"Your bathroom is next door—you'll have privacy. My room and bath are on the other side."

Carrie unpacked a few things from her overnight bag and after freshening up, joined her hostess in the kitchen.

Mrs. Dillard pulled a small lasagna casserole out of the oven and with a depreciating smile murmured, "I hope you don't mind. It's not homemade. I don't do a lot of cooking these days."

"I'm sure it will be wonderful, Mrs. Dillard."

"Call me Norma, dear. You can help me with the salad."

Carrie broke up the lettuce and sliced a tomato. Mrs. Dillard sprinkled on some parmesan cheese and tossed the salad in a bowl with some Italian dressing.

"How do you and my mother know each other, Norma?" Carrie asked as they sat down at the small kitchen table.

"Well, I was a friend of your grandmother's. I knew your mother when she was a girl. She's been kind enough to keep in touch with me over the years and usually stops to see me when she comes through Sacramento."

Norma asked the blessing over the food. As they began to eat, she looked at Carrie's left hand. "That's a lovely ring, dear. When is the wedding?"

"July. That's why I'm hurrying home. There's so much to do.'

"My, you don't have much time. What do your folks think of your fiancé?"

Carrie sighed. "They haven't met him yet. He's coming up in a week to meet them." She described Andrew and enthusiastically talked about the antique business. She made sure Norma knew Andrew had taken her to church.

Norma listened quietly, her face thoughtful. "I wish you happiness, dear." She started to say something else but seemed to think better of it and just patted Carrie's hand.

It was only seven thirty, but Carrie was becoming aware of just how tired she was. At least she had eight and a half of the thirteen hour trip behind her.

"Now when you need to, you just go on to bed."

Norma was a *Wheel of Fortune* and *Jeopardy* fan and they watched both programs together. She was also a Bill Gaither fan and she and Carrie enjoyed a music video after the TV shows. Carrie's eyes were getting heavy and she caught herself dozing off a couple of times.

With a smile, Norma shooed her off to bed.

"I'm an early riser. What time would you like breakfast?"

"You've been so nice, I hate to impose on you for breakfast too."

Norma gave her a stern look over her glasses. "One of the blessings of life is being able to help others. God brought you my way today and I'm glad for the company. I was happy to help your mother out. She has done so many nice things for me."

Properly chastened, Carrie gave Norma a warm hug. "Then thank you. I do appreciate breaking up the trip."

"Good. Now what time would you like breakfast?"

"Does 7:30 sound okay to you? I want to hopefully get home by around noon."

"That's perfect, dear." I'll see you then." As Carrie started toward the bedroom, Norma called out, "and there are fresh towels in the bathroom."

She tried calling Andrew again, and this time he answered. There seemed like a lot of noise in the background.

"Where are you, Andrew? I can hardly hear you."

"I'm at a restaurant, babe. The reception isn't good here."

And where is here? She was afraid to ask and after a brief conversation punctuated by static, he told her to drive safely, promised to call in the next day or two, and hung up. She resisted the impulse to throw the phone across the room. What was the matter with her? She sighed. She was probably just tired.

She took a warm shower and let the soothing water flow over her shoulders and body. The last thing she remembered was crawling between soft cotton sheets.

Carrie was up before her alarm went off at 7:00. She put on a pair of jeans and a comfortable T-shirt, brushed her hair and made sure she'd collected all her toiletries from the bathroom. Then she went out to the kitchen.

Norma had poured a glass of orange juice, and the smell of coffee permeated the room.

"Are you a coffee drinker, dear?"

"A cup of coffee would be great."

Carrie wasn't used to big breakfasts, but didn't want to hurt Norma's feelings, and when scrambled eggs, two slices of bacon, and a small muffin were place in front of her, she beamed and ate everything.

She still had several hours of driving and after giving her hostess a hug, she thanked her for her hospitality, got in her car and drove off. Just outside the park she called her folks to let them know she was on her way again.

"Mrs. Dillard was so nice, Mom. Thanks for working that out. I didn't realize how tired I was until I got there. I'll see you in a couple of hours. I should be there by noon or so."

"Good, darling, I'll have lunch waiting for you."

As she drove, Carrie thought about her apartment. She didn't have time to sort through all her things. She'd dispose of the larger items later. It was something she needed to take time to do and there just wasn't time. Right now she had her hands full getting ready for her wedding. She thought about the last conversation with her mom. Her folks hadn't asked about Andrew again, but she knew her father. He'd wait until she was home. She shook off the slight feeling of apprehension that tugged once again at the back of her mind and concentrated on the road ahead.

As she drove through Redding and started up into the mountains, she took a deep breath as the scent of the tall Douglas and Ponderosa pines added their pungent scent to the spring air. Along the side of the road, the scotch broom were clumped in splashes of bright golden color, and here and there the wild lilac lay in patches like small throw rugs of lavender tossed on the hillsides.

Driving the familiar roads was comforting. When someone from their community had to go down to the city it was referred to as "driving the mountain." Five years before she had "driven the mountain" on a bus headed for college. She returned the same way during vacation and holidays for the first year, but soon the need for a part-time job consumed her extra time. Her trips home dwindled to the few long weekends she was fortunate to get off to make the long trip on the bus. Her parents finally gifted her with the little Mustang.

She glanced at her ring. "I'm engaged." She could hardly believe it as she said the words out loud. She waited for the euphoria, but there was only a sense of apprehension. She stepped harder on the accelerator.

The huge diamond caught the sun and glittered and as she drove, she found herself considering the small but elegant engagement party the weekend before graduation at the Van Zant's beautiful home overlooking the ocean. A swarm of people and faces she could scarcely remember. The women, beautiful and casually elegant in their designer clothes came from a world Carrie had never known. As Andrew propelled her along from one group to another, the women evaluated her over their drinks and purred like so many sleek cats.

"Darling, so nice to see you again, is this the little bride-to-be? How sweet."

"Well, we get to meet you at last, such a clever girl to capture our Andrew."

"You naughty boy, I was planning on marrying you myself."

"This is so sudden, Andrew. Wherever did you find her?" The tone of voice suggested that perhaps it was under a rock.

Though it was all said lightly, Carrie felt like an outsider. She kept a smile on her face, nodding her head politely as she was drawn from group to group. They didn't seem to expect her to say much of anything. She tried to remember names, but, it was a daunting task.

The scene faded as she approached the bridge over the river and slowed down to watch a couple of mallard ducks swimming along the far side. She gazed at the rushing water and to her delight, an otter popped up out of the water and stared at her with soulful eyes.

Crossing the bridge she followed a winding gravel road to a driveway where a weather-beaten sign said "Dickson Hollow." She turned in toward home and her heart lifted as she came in sight of the sprawling two-story house with redwood siding. It had weathered through the years. Her mother's Ford Bronco II was in the carport and next to it was her father's gray Silverado truck. Carrie's heart lifted when she saw a red CDF truck. Had her dad taken time off work to be there when she got home? Two unfamiliar cars caught her eye—a Lexus and an older Volkswagen Jetta parked near the trailer they used for a guest house. *Company?* She pulled into her portion of the carport and got out to stretch.

The back door opened and her parents strode toward her. A joyful series of barks greeted her as Nubbins, her black Labrador, rushed past them. With his tail wagging and a light in his eyes, he bounded out to her, skidded to a stop, and sat, his body trembling with anticipation as he waited expectantly for her caress on his head.

Was it only yesterday that Nubbins was a fat little puppy with a red bow around his neck, licking her face on her tenth birthday? Now, stroking his soft fur, she noted the gray hairs on his muzzle. Nubbins was getting old.

"Carrie dear, I couldn't wait until you got here." Helen Dickson gave her daughter a big hug. She wore a pair of jeans and a rust-colored cotton plaid shirt. Her auburn hair was tied back with a bright paisley scarf. Her complexion needed little makeup, even in her forties and her one indulgence was a dab of lipstick.

"Well, Cousin," drawled a familiar voice. "Looks like you've done all right for yourself." She touched Carrie's shoulders lightly and kissed the air by her left ear, the expected gesture.

"Linda, what a surprise."

Linda's beige silk pants and matching blouse fit her trim figure. Gold earrings dangled from her ears and ropes of gold chain hung about her neck. Gold bracelets made tinkling sounds as she moved her arms. On anyone else they might have looked gaudy, but Linda wore the jewelry, as she did everything else, with style. Her honey-colored hair was drawn back in a severe and elegant bun.

For a fleeting moment, Carrie wondered if Linda ever let it blow in the wind.

Linda always appeared relaxed and casual, but her large hazel eyes, accented by perfectly plucked brows, seldom missed anything, especially an opportunity to take center stage.

Carrie realized the Lexus must belong to her cousin. Linda was a buyer for a fashionable chain of women's stores and it occurred to Carrie that her cousin was doing better than she thought.

Carrie's dad, "Bear" Dickson, so named for his size and the profusion of hair on his back and arms, smiled broadly as he gave Carrie a warm hug. His light brown hair was streaked with gray at the temples. When he smiled, little lines crinkled in the corners of his eyes.

He stepped back, gave Carrie a stern look, and got to the point. "When did you say this young man was coming?"

"Next weekend. He's very anxious to meet my family."

"This is all pretty sudden, Cricket. We've never even met Andrew and you're engaged already. I would have thought he'd come to me first. Maybe that's too old fashioned for these modern young men. We just want to know more about this Andrew Van Zant who's swept our little girl off her feet."

She beamed at him. "I know you'll love Andrew, Daddy."

Her father just nodded his head.

"What I want to see is this ring," Linda interrupted to grab Carrie's left hand and hold the diamond up to the light.

"Well," she breathed, "I think we're going to need our sunglasses."

"It's beautiful, Carrie." Her mother looked at the ring from all sides. "Did you design it together?"

"No, actually, it was his grandmother's. Isn't that wonderful?" Carrie smiled brightly.

"Well, if you ever decide to hock the ring you could buy a small house," Linda put in dryly.   Carrie gently withdrew her hand from their scrutiny

Ever practical, Helen took charge. "Let me call Scott to bring in all the baggage. Good heavens, I can remember when she came home with only one battered suitcase."

"Scott?" Carrie looked at her mother. Could it be who she thought it was?

CHAPTER EIGHT

*H*ELEN PUT AN arm around Carrie's waist. "You remember Scott Spencer, don't you? He used to give you a ride to school once in a while. He's a teacher down in Napa Valley now, home for the summer. He's staying with us."

Scott. Six feet two inches, with dark wavy hair and deep-set blue eyes, and a way of looking at you when he gave you his full attention that made every guy at school his friend and every girl, including Carrie, a bowl of jelly.

She'd had an enormous crush on him but he was two years ahead of her. The best quarterback their high school football team ever had. Scott was well-liked but rarely went to any of the parties and didn't date the popular girls. As she recalled, he didn't drink or smoke either. He never made an issue of it and neither did anyone else. During the long, languid summers she and her friends spent at Whiskeytown Lake, Scott headed to Mexico or some such place with a group from his church to build something.

The Spencers lived at the top of the hill, and Carrie thought back to the shy young girl she was, waiting at the bus stop and hoping he'd stop and offer her a ride. When he did, she was too tongue-tied to respond to his attempt at light conversation. They rode in silence. Though it was years ago, she suddenly felt the same embarrassment she felt then.

Oh yes, she remembered Scott Spencer.

"His parents are remodeling," her mother was saying, "there is just not room in their motorhome for three. I told Scott he was welcome to stay in the guest house all summer until he goes back to Napa."

The "guest house" was a twenty-eight foot trailer Helen had gotten from a friend and renovated. A couple of large pots of red geraniums stood on either side of the door and Helen painted a whimsical sign, denoting its use, that hung at an angle on the side of the trailer. She and Carrie reupholstered the dinette area and added a small comfortable couch and chair. A bright blue bedspread and curtains added a feminine but not too frilly touch.

Linda folded her arms and eyed Carrie, her husky voice almost a purr. "Since you are obviously taken, you won't mind if I entertain our guest?"

Carrie waved a hand at her cousin. "Feel free." Linda carried a torch for Scott when they were in school, but though he was friendly, as he was with everyone, he didn't encourage her.

Just then, the object of their conversation stepped out of the trailer and strolled toward them. A pair of faded jeans and a light blue T-shirt enhanced his well-built physique. His hair was still damp from a shower. Carrie watched him approach and realized she was glad to see him.

He stood and studied her, his head tilted to one side.

"Welcome home," he said softly. It almost seemed to be a question.

She put on a bright smile. "Hello Scott, it's good to see you again."

Helen waved a hand at the luggage. Just then a cell phone went off and Carrie's father flipped it open.

"Yes?" He nodded and frowned. "Can it wait? My daughter just arrived home." He listened again. "I see. All right, I'm on my way."

Helen turned, "Will you be home for dinner later?"

He shook his head. "There's a small brush fire by Rush Creek. As dry as things are right now, we can't take any chances. I'll be back as soon as I can—just save me some of that pot roast." He turned to Carrie. "We'll talk later, okay, Cricket?" She smiled back and nodded.

Carrie glanced at the look of resignation on her mother's face. Her father supervised a fire crew for the Department of Forestry, and they had long ago resigned themselves to missed dinners and special events when a fire reared its ugly head.

Helen turned to Scott. "The prodigal has returned. We need your help."

He grinned at the open trunk. "I can see that." And with little effort, he tucked a smaller suitcase under each arm and with each hand picked up the two larger suitcases she'd borrowed from friends. Carrie had grabbed her purse and small cosmetics case. Her mother gazed at the rest of the things Carrie had stuffed in the back seat of the car. "We'll get all that later, dear. You'll want to freshen up after that long drive."

As they started toward the house her mother beamed at Scott. "Her room is all ready. Carrie, you can show him where to put those suitcases."

Leading the way upstairs, Carrie was aware of his eyes appraising her. They reached the bedroom she'd had since she was a child, and as she opened the door he glanced around. The canopy over the bed and the ruffled bedspread were white organza with tiny pink and blue flowers. Several stuffed animals were stacked on the bed against the pillows.

Carrie frowned. It had always been her haven, but now she saw it through the eyes of her new found sophistication. It was a little girl's room.

She waved a hand. "Just put them down there," indicating the center of the room.

She looked around. "I need to do something about my room. It's the same as it's always been."

Scott gazed at her intently. "And, are you?" he asked.

Feeling awkward, she looked away. Then, drawing herself up she gave him a polite smile. "Thank you for bringing my bags up."

At Scott's arched eyebrows she regretted her tone of voice. He tipped two fingers to his head like a salute and to her acute embarrassment turned and walked to the door, pausing briefly to look back at her. His dark eyes were unreadable as he noted the ring on her finger.

The moment he was gone she flung her hands up in the air. Now why on earth had she talked to Scott like that? He was a friend. Things just weren't going the way she expected. She unpacked some of her things and changed into a pair of tan shorts and a soft green T-shirt, feeling a little more comfortable.

When she came downstairs there was a sudden hush of conversation as two pairs of eyes looked up at her. Scott was nowhere in sight.

Linda smiled archly. "My, whatever did you say to Scott? He looked a bit grim when he left."

Carrie brushed an imaginary piece of lint off her sleeve. "I can't imagine. We hardly talked at all."

"Scott is going to have lunch with his parents. He'll join us for dinner." As her mother led the way to the dining room, Carrie glanced back at Linda with raised eyebrows. They usually ate at the oak table in the large kitchen. Linda only smiled and shrugged. "After all, you're moving up in the world."

Carrie's mother had made her famous Mexican serendipity salad which consisted of whatever salad greens and things were in the refrigerator along with hamburger and pinto beans spooned on top with a dollop of sour cream. It was Carrie's favorite on a hot day.

The midday meal flowed with small talk as Helen filled Carrie and Linda in on recent community happenings and other mundane topics. But then, sitting back, pleasantly full, Helen turned to Carrie with a smile of anticipation.

"Now darling, when is the wedding date? How much time do we have?"

"Andrew wants to be married on the Fourth of July. He said he wanted to have a "bang up" wedding just before his thirtieth birthday."

They looked at her blankly.

"This is certainly happening fast, Carrie. That isn't much time. It's the first of June now. I'll have to call Pastor Richards to see if the Community Church is available on a holiday. Oh, good heavens, did you remember the all-church picnic is that day?"

Carrie took a deep breath. She might as well get it over with. "You don't have to worry about that, Mother. The Van Zants have arranged for the wedding to be at their church in La Jolla. They felt it would have more room for, ah, everyone. A caterer has been hired, and everything." She gave her mother and cousin a tentative smile.

There was an astonished silence. "The whole thing is already arranged?" Helen asked.

"Everything." Carrie looked from one face to the other.

Linda rolled her eyes, "What did you expect? Our little Carrie is moving into high society." She tilted her head and smirked. "I hope they don't mind if any of your poor relatives attend."

"Now hush, Linda," Helen intervened, "I'm sure this is all new to Carrie. We will help in any way we can, won't we?" Helen looked pointedly at her niece, but Linda only shrugged.

Helen, recovering from her surprise, attempted to hide her disappointment.

"Oh. Well that's very nice of them, isn't it? I'm sure with the people they know, they would want to make it elegant." She thought for a moment and her face lit up.

"What about your dress? Have you looked at any yet? We can go down—" At the look on Carrie's face, she chewed on her lower lip and was silent.

Her mother's hopeful tone made Carrie cringe, but with a rueful smile she nodded.

"Andrew had me go to the bridal salon a few days ago."

Carrie had dutifully gone to her appointment and the sales-woman, evidently properly coached, discouraged the rather plain, simple dresses Carrie started to look at. She brought out a stunning creation of French lace with thousands of seed pearls. It was the most beautiful dress Carrie had ever seen. When it was slipped over her head it rustled and shimmered with tiny lights. She almost didn't recognize the girl who looked back at her in the mirror. When the tiara was placed on her head with its cascading veil, she had no words. She could only look at the glittering creation and nod. The saleswoman smiled benignly and helped her off with the dress.

"We'll just box this right up and send it to Mr. Van Zant."

Carrie started to ask why it wasn't going to her apartment, but then realized she wasn't the one paying for the dress. She wondered how much a dress like that cost but was too embarrassed to ask.

As well as she could, Carrie described the wedding dress to her family. Her mother sat open-mouthed and Linda looked smug.

"Unless I miss my guess, that dress is worth several thousand dollars." She sat back, enjoying the startled look on Carrie's face. "I wonder what they've picked out for me." She turned to her aunt. "Carrie asked me to be her maid of honor."

Helen gave a half-hearted nod of approval and Linda waved a hand. "We're going to do a bridal shower that will be the talk of the town."

Helen looked up from her thoughts. "A shower? Yes, of course, a lovely idea, Linda." She turned hopefully to Carrie.

"Oh, that would be wonderful."

Her mother looked visibly relieved.

"Well, I'm glad there is something we can do," Linda murmured dryly. "Give me some paper and a pen. Let's get started. I'll host the shower—you know the mother of the bride is not supposed to give it."

Helen nodded. That was true. Soon the two women were deep in plans, arrangements, and invitation lists. After agreeing on the date, two weeks hence, Carrie sat quietly listening. Linda took charge and had definite ideas of what she wanted. Carrie got up and stretched. Listening to the murmur of voices, she was glad her mother would at least have a part in the arrangements. She shook her head. She herself hadn't had much say in the arrangements either. She'd tried tentatively to make some additional suggestions to Andrew's father but while Dietrich Van Zant nodded kindly and listened, he'd patted her on the shoulder as if she were a child to be mollified. He ignored her suggestions and went ahead making arrangements as he saw fit.

"You must understand, my dear, that there are certain social obligations, ah, in keeping with our position. Now don't worry your pretty head about a thing. Everything is well in hand."

At least she had been able to choose her maid of honor. She knew it had to be Linda. While she'd made several friends in college and there were friends from high school, it would be hard to pick one without hurting someone's feelings. They would understand about Linda, and it would keep the family peace. As it was, there would be four bridesmaids.

Carrie wondered if she should be upset about not being able to plan her wedding, and yet, as she pictured herself floating down the aisle to Andrew in the fairytale dress, she decided to leave it alone. The most important thing was that she and Andrew would be together as man and wife. She no longer asked about the wedding preparations. Evidently all she had to do was be there.

Now, as she looked at the two women with their heads together, she smiled ruefully. It appeared she wasn't needed to plan the shower either. She motioned to Nubbins and quietly slipped outside.

She went down the stepping stones and footpath that went down to the river. Nubbins ran ahead along the bank sniffing and savoring rabbit and deer smells.

Watching him, she absentmindedly tossed small pebbles into the rippling waters. She should be on top of the world and yet, something was wrong.

"This is a good place to think about things."

With a start, she turned to see Scott watching her. She had been so absorbed in her thoughts she hadn't heard him come down the path. He moved toward her with an easy masculine grace. There was a sense of strength about him. Carrie was very much aware of him as a man and not the boy of her high school days.

She smiled tentatively, turning back to the river. Perhaps he regretted their earlier meeting. He was trying to be friendly? Why was it so hard to talk to him?

Scott reached down and scratched Nubbins behind the ears. "Will you be married in the Community Church?"

She turned back. "No, the Van Zants' church in San Diego." For some reason she felt the need to explain. "They've been members there a long time." She didn't add that while the Van Zants were members, they seldom attended. It was only for functions like the wedding that they took advantage of their church membership.

"I see." It was said as if he'd read her thoughts. "How do you like the minister there?"

She tossed a last pebble. "I've never met him. The Sunday Andrew and I went, he was out of town. They had a guest speaker." She could have bitten her tongue. Now she was telling Scott that she and Andrew had only been to church once together.

"Will you and Andrew meet with the minister before the wedding?"

"No, I don't think so, but he's a man of God. He's qualified to perform the ceremony."

Scott put his hands in his pockets and stared out at the river for a moment before looking earnestly at her. "Maybe it just doesn't seem right, getting married without considering what part God is going to play in your marriage."

"What do you mean? We're going to be married in the church, before God. And I do believe in God, Scott."

"I know you do, Carrie. What about Andrew? "

She bristled. "Well, of course, Andrew believes in God." Suddenly she didn't want to talk about God anymore. That was something she and Andrew didn't discuss. She'd brought up the subject a couple of times, but Andrew had deftly turned to another topic. By now Scott's steady gaze was more than disconcerting.

"So, I hear you are a teacher now. Where do you teach?"

Scott frowned. She gathered that wasn't what he wanted to talk about, but he accepted the diversion. "I teach at a small Christian high school down in the valley—physical education, a few history classes. I also coach the football team."

"Do you like being a teacher? You were very good at football. I'm sure you make a good coach."

He accepted the compliment with a shrug. "Yes, I like being a teacher. It's what God called me to do. And, of course, I enjoy the coaching."

"God called you to teach?" She tried to make it sound casual, "How do you know that?"

He chuckled. "God speaks to us in many ways, Carrie. Sometimes you just know in your heart that this is the vocation He's chosen for you. That this is the direction your life is to go."

"And if it is not the direction?"

"He lets you know. There's no peace in your spirit and obstacles seem to pop up in your way. My mom always said she wished God would put out neon signs, but I guess there are other signs that tell us we are going the wrong way."

Carrie thought of the direction her life was going. While it all seemed so exciting and overwhelming, she had an unsettled feeling sometimes. She wondered what it would be like to have God speak to her. She shrugged off the thoughts and turned back to the river.

"The river is higher than usual."

He came to stand a little closer. "They're sending the salmon fry down to the sea, or at least that is what they tell us. Seems like we had a whole lot more fish in the river before all this river management."

They looked at the river for a moment in silence, then he glanced at her.

"All these wedding plans seem rather sudden. Will we get a chance to meet your fiancé before the wedding?"

There he goes again, a one-track mind. She lifted her chin and faced him, smiling. "Yes, he will be here next weekend to meet my family. I can hardly wait until he gets here."

His lip twitched with a whisper of a smile. Was he mocking her? She started back up the path past him. "I'd better get back." Nubbins ran off after a squirrel and she let him go.

"I'll walk with you." He strode easily beside her but neither spoke as they headed toward the house. Scott stopped as if he would say more but thought better of it.

"I'll see you later, Carrie." He tipped his fingers to his head as he'd done before and went on to the trailer.

She stood watching him for a moment. He certainly had a lot of nerve, the way he quizzed her. When Scott stopped and glanced back, she hurried into the house.

The bridal shower was organized to Linda's satisfaction and she'd gone upstairs to change clothes. Helen moved around the kitchen, cleaning up after lunch.

"There's a guest list on the table, honey. See if there is anyone you want to add."

Carrie added the names of two friends from college and another friend from high school.

Putting an arm companionably through hers, her mother drew Carrie out to the large porch that ran the length of the house. They settled in the shade of an umbrella in comfortable redwood chairs with bright yellow-flowered cushions.

"We haven't had much of a chance to talk. I'm happy for you, dear, but I guess the way things seemed to be moving so fast, it took me by surprise."

"I hope it's all right, I mean about our not getting married here in the Community Church. It was kind of arranged before I knew about it."

"Of course, darling, it's just that I was wondering, the haste of the wedding and all..." Her voice trailed away as she searched her daughter's face.

Then Carrie understood. She blushed and for a moment looked down at her hands. So that's what they've been wondering. Shaking her head she looked her mother in the eyes. "I don't have to get married, Mother. Andrew just said that now that he'd found the right girl he wasn't going to let her slip away. He said he couldn't handle a long engagement."

Carrie could make light of the thought now, but remembering back to an occasion in her apartment, she realized things could have been different. Andrew had felt very amorous one evening after bringing her home and wanted to make love to her. She tried to make him understand that she wanted their wedding night to be special. It had been instilled in her from the time she was a young girl.

"Darling, we're going to be married. Don't tell me you are a prude," he murmured as he nuzzled her ear. He kissed her again on the throbbing pulse in her throat, and she felt her resolve crumbling. It took all of her willpower to push him away.

He sighed heavily, got up, and, giving her a look that left her feeling hollow inside, walked out, slamming the door. She cried herself to sleep that night.

In the morning Andrew called her and apologized. He was truly repentant, and to emphasize his apology he sent two dozen red roses as he'd done once before. Nothing more was said about the incident.

Now she faced her mother brightly. "I know you'll love Andrew, Mother. He's charming and witty and really likes people. I know he's caused some concern to his father, not settling down and all, but I'm sure he's ready now."

"Have you talked about a family?"

"Andrew wants to wait a while. He's not used to children. He was an only child, like me, and he says he needs to get adjusted to the idea of being married first, maybe in a few years."

"Of course, dear, I understand." But there was no conviction in her mother's voice.

CHAPTER NINE

*H*ER MOTHER RETURNED to the kitchen and Carrie went to finish unpacking. As she began to take things out of her suitcases she wondered why she packed so much. With Andrew she learned to be prepared for anything he decided to do.

Andrew's friends lived a completely different lifestyle. She didn't play bridge or golf, and even though she'd played some tennis, it helped little to integrate her into the group.

Not being active in an auxiliary or philanthropic group, she tried to keep up with the conversations but found herself hiding the fact that she was raised in a small mountain community. Andrew seemed to appear just in time to move her on to another group.

"We'll have to talk later, dear," a woman said as Carrie turned away.

"Yes, of course. Nice talking with you." She never felt so phony.

Now, as she hung the clothes quickly in her closet, she felt relieved she didn't have to dress for dinner at home, one benefit of living in the country. She wondered if they would be eating in the dining room again. Her mother told her that there had been quite a discussion over that issue. Linda insisted that with the society life Carrie was now used to, they needed to use the dining room.

Helen had argued that the kitchen had always been good enough when Carrie was home before. In the end, Linda won out. Now, with Linda and Scott staying at the house, they would have to eat in the dining room anyway.

Sitting down on the floor, cross-legged, Carrie surveyed her bookshelves. There might be some books she would like to take with her. She pulled them out one by one, savoring the titles. It was like getting acquainted with old friends—*My Friend Flicka, Black Beauty,* a couple of old romance books by Grace Livingston Hill. She loved the English writer, Rosamond Piltcher, for her wonderful characters. Then, there was a lovely illustrated copy of *Little Women* and several books of poetry. Her favorite book was *The Song of the Cardinal* by Gene Stratton-Porter. It was an old book her mother had found in a second-hand shop and given to her on her twelfth birthday. Carrie looked at the faded green cloth cover with the picture of a red cardinal on it. It was a tender love story about a bird searching for a mate, so poignantly written the story still brought tears to her eyes. Perhaps she ought to leave them here for now. Maybe she'd have a daughter one day who would enjoy these.

As she reached for the next book, it was the small copy of the New Testament given her in Sunday school. She sighed. Church had been such a big part of her life, and yet college had been difficult. Many of her part-time jobs involved working on Sunday. She'd finally found a little church not far from her apartment and went when she could.

Scott's words down by the river played over in her mind. Had she really given any thought to what part God would play in her marriage?

Then a portion of Scripture came to mind. *Don't be unequally yoked.*

Questions chased themselves around in her head.

"You're wanted for dinner, cousin." Carrie jumped and turned to see Linda leaning lazily against the doorway. She was beautiful as always in a pair of designer jeans and a soft lavender silk shirt. No shorts or T-shirts for Linda.

"Mom called you several times. Dad will be a little late but the fire is under control."

"Oh, that's good. I was absorbed in looking through my books. I didn't hear her."

"Obviously." Linda stepped into the room and gave a disdainful look at the bedspread and stuffed animals. "A little out of date, don't you think?"

Carrie smarted under Linda's withering look.

"Well, I'm not here much." She looked down at the Bible in her hand.

Linda's brows lifted quizzically when she saw the Bible.

Carrie looked up earnestly. "Do you go to church anymore?"

Her cousin looked startled. "Once in a while when I'm here at home, mostly because your folks would have apoplexy if I didn't. What made you ask that, for heaven's sake?"

Carrie looked back down at her Bible. *For heaven's sake. Maybe that was why she wanted to know.* "I just wondered," she offered lamely.

"Well let's not get off on the subject of religion, cousin. I get enough of that from your mother." Linda smiled archly. "We have a guest for dinner, in case you've forgotten. I'm sure he's starved, and so am I."

Self-consciously Carrie placed the Bible back on the shelf and got up to quickly change clothes. Scott was joining them for dinner. Well, she would be polite even if he did rub her the wrong way. There was no need to let her parents know there was any friction.

Scott wore a pair of dark slacks and a short-sleeved light gray cotton shirt. The thought crossed Carrie's mind that he would look handsome in anything he wore. Linda smiled her most alluring smile, tucked her arm in his, and led him to the dinner table.

A great-smelling pot roast and vegetables, and sliced beefsteak tomatoes from Helen's garden arranged in a pretty dish were placed in the center of the table, ready for the family to begin eating.

The sound of a truck coming down the driveway announced the arrival of Mike Dickson, and a few moments later, he strode into the dining room looking hungry.

"I knew you'd make it," Helen smiled indulgently and lifted her cheek for his kiss.

Carrie found herself facing Scott across the table. She smiled sweetly at him as they sat down. As they bowed their heads, Linda sighed loudly.

Mike gave her a piercing look and then turned to Scott. "Son, would you do us the honor of saying grace?" Carrie gave her father a puzzled glance. He usually always said grace.

"Be glad to."

Scott's voice was low and reverent. "Lord, we thank You for Your wonderful bounty that we enjoy tonight. Thank You for the family gathered here this evening and for bringing Carrie and Linda home safely. Bless, we pray, Lord, the hands that have so kindly prepared this food that it may nourish our bodies. We ask these things in the name of Your Son, our Lord and Savior, Jesus Christ. Amen."

Carrie listened to the prayer thoughtfully. Scott and God seemed to be on intimate terms.

Linda gave Scott another winning smile. "Well, now that the important preliminaries are taken care of, how about passing the roast beef?"

He smiled pleasantly, handed her the platter, and glanced at Carrie. Their eyes met briefly. The intensity of his gaze made her self-conscious and she hastily occupied herself with filling her plate.

"How do you like Mrs. Van Zant?" Linda's question caught her unaware.

"Mrs. Van Zant?"

"Surely Andrew has a mother," Linda drawled, "just who is doing all this wedding planning?"

They all looked at Carrie expectantly.

"Andrew's mother died when he was ten. His father has made all the arrangements." She shrugged. "He knew who to call and everything." She stopped. It wasn't coming out right.

Surprisingly, Scott came to her rescue. "He sounds like a fine person. I'm sure he's very pleased with his son's choice of a bride."

She shot him a quick glance of gratitude. There was an uncomfortable silence until Helen jumped into the conversational void.

"I had to almost double the chicken wire around the outside of the garden this year. The rabbits got my first planting of corn, ate the new shoots down to the nubs. I had to replace eight rows!" She looked so outraged and it had been such a sudden shift in topics that they all found themselves laughing. Carrie relaxed again.

Scott smiled at Helen. "At least the deer can't jump the fence now that you put up those two extra rows of wire around the posts."

"Yes, thanks to you. I thought I would lose the whole garden."

They all looked at Scott who shrugged modestly. "Deer can jump a six-foot fence from a dead standstill. Now the height is eight feet. So far they haven't tried it."

"In any case, I appreciate the suggestion and the help with the wire," Helen told him warmly.

Carrie turned to her father. "How bad was the fire?"

"It was starting to get going. The brush is so dry right now. Luckily we got to it in time. The Joneses almost lost part of their barn, though." He turned to Scott. "Are you going to man the lookout tower again this summer?"

"I'll do a week. I'm trying to help my folks get the house finished before their anniversary party in August."

Mike nodded, "Always a good thing to help your folks."

Occasionally during dinner Carrie sensed Scott's eyes on her and considered his question down at the river. Just what would Andrew say if she suggested that they meet the minister before the wedding for counseling? Even as the question entered her mind, she knew the answer. They had only gone that one Sunday so Andrew could show her the church. They hadn't been back.

"Speaking of your parent's home, Scott, how is the remodeling coming along?" Helen was scooping vanilla ice cream into dishes of warm apple cobbler.

"The house should be finished in about a month." Scott turned to Linda.

"How's your job going?"

Linda's face lit up with a pleased smile to suddenly have his undivided attention since she had been trying to charm him all through dinner. She began to share about her new position, her new boss, and a co-worker who was giving her problems.

"He not only wants my job, but he's quite willing to step on my head to get there. He undermines me every chance he gets. When he makes a mistake, he tries to get the boss to think I did it. A real worm!" Linda was vehement.

"I'm sure if you are doing a good job, your boss will see that man's actions for what they are, Linda."

Linda's face brightened. She smiled alluringly and leaned toward him, brushing her arm against his.

Scott remained pleasant as he turned to the rest of them. Helen was asking about his school.

"It's small but nice. The kids are a little crazy sometimes and can be a real challenge, but I enjoy it." He told them about some of the students he had worked with the previous year. Obviously he liked what he was doing and Carrie couldn't help but contrast Scott's calm demeanor, at peace with himself and his faith, with Andrew's constant moving among his social circle. She looked down at her ring and the shadows were once again pushed back by its brilliance. *I love Andrew, I do. And he loves me.* She was not aware of how her chin lifted when she decided something in her mind, but caught a strange look on Scott's face.

Carrie turned quickly in her mother's direction. "By the way, what's happening down at the bookshop?"

"Well, let's see, we have two book clubs going, one on Monday evening for men, mostly non-fiction, and a women's group meeting on Wednesday mornings while the kids are in school. They read a little of everything. We have a children's story time on Thursday afternoons, and on Friday nights I've started poetry readings. Oh, and I'll have to show you the wonderful collection of old children's books I just acquired. Found them in a second-hand store. The owner just wanted to get rid of them, can you imagine?" Helen's eyes sparkled as they always did when she was excited about something.

"Your mother has quite the nose for a book bargain." Mike beamed at her, and Carrie was struck again by the wonderful relationship she'd seen between her parents through the years.

Helen began collecting dishes from the table and looked pointedly at Linda. Carrie suspected she planned to make herself scarce. Linda always hated doing chores.

Linda gave Scott a bright smile. "We'd love to have your help in the kitchen, Scott."

"He has a meeting, Linda." Mike reached out to shake Scott's hand. "Nice to see you, son, come again soon."

"Sorry to eat and run, Mrs. Dickson."

"No problem, honey, I understand."

Mike turned to his niece. "I think while you and your mom are doing dishes maybe Carrie and I could talk."

Linda rolled her eyes and Carrie was embarrassed to have Scott turn to look at her.

"Sure, Dad, I'd like that."

As they got up from the table, Carrie started to clear dishes. Maybe she and her father could talk a little later. He came around and with a wink, tucked her arm in his. No such reprieve.

"You'll get plenty of chances to do dishes while you're here, young lady, don't worry." Her father headed for the study. She had nothing to hide or confess, so why was she reluctant to talk to her father?

Scott turned to Carrie. "Looks like you'll be busy this next couple of weeks, but maybe I can show you what we've done to the house."

"That would be nice, Scott, but I just don't know how much free time I'll have, you know, with the wedding and all."

Scott was silent a moment. Then, although he spoke quietly, there seemed almost a note of sarcasm to his voice. "Yes, I imagine that would give you a lot to think about."

He studied her and she found herself once more looking away. Why couldn't she look him in the eye? Linda moved quickly to go with him, insisting on seeing him to the door.

Carrie sighed. That was stupid. *Why did she and Scott always seem to be on the wrong foot with each other?*

Her father closed the door to the den and settled in his easy chair. "We're happy for you, Cricket, if you're happy. I'd just like to know more about your young man. Tell me about him."

Carrie perched on the chair opposite him. She told him everything positive she could think of about Andrew, his articles in the school paper, and being the editor, meeting his father, and ending with the wonderful engagement dinner at La Rouge.

"Sounds like they enjoy a busy social life. How do you feel about that?"

He still hadn't asked the one question she knew was at the back of his mind.

"I'm a little nervous, Daddy. Sometimes I feel a little out of place." She brightened. "I'm learning though. Andrew really helps me a lot."

"I'm sure he does." He paused.

Here it comes. She braced herself and waited.

"Does Andrew go to church with you, Carrie?"

"He took me to his church." Well, that part was true. "I'm sure he believes in God."

"But he's not a Christian?"

She took a deep breath and let it out slowly. "No, Daddy, he isn't."

"I see. How do you think that will affect your marriage?"

"Well, I believe he will respect my beliefs, and I know that in time he'll see his need to make that decision."

Her father was silent. He looked at Carrie and for a brief moment she saw a look of sadness come over his face.

"But Daddy, you and Mom weren't Christians when you married." It was grasping at a straw and she knew it.

"That's right, honey, both of us didn't know the Lord, but when one person is a Christian and marries someone who doesn't know Christ, there can be problems."

Her chin lifted defensively. "We can face those problems, Daddy."

"I know you believe that, Cricket, but what if he tells you he doesn't want you to go to church anymore, or ridicules your beliefs?"

"Andrew wouldn't do that."

"Perhaps not, maybe I'm just playing devil's advocate here. Your mother and I had some rough years before you were born. We almost parted ways. Then she found Christ and the change in her was so profound, I wanted to experience what she'd found. It was the turning point in our marriage when I walked down to the altar one night."

"You've had a wonderful marriage, Daddy, and I want to have a wonderful marriage too."

"Our marriage is based on putting God first."

"I love him, Daddy."

"I know, honey, I know." He sighed. "Well, we look forward to meeting this young man. If you love him, we'll just love him too."

She threw her arms around her father's neck and hugged him. "I know you'll feel better once you meet him."

He hugged her back. "How about seeing if you can help your mother and Linda in the kitchen? Linda's got to be driving her crazy by now."

She laughed, relieved that they had talked. She was sure once her parents met Andrew they would like him—wouldn't they? As she left her father's den she saw him reach for his Bible.

The kitchen was cleaned up and the dishwasher was running. Her mother and Linda were watching the news.

Carrie wandered out on the porch. A soft muzzle against her hand told her Nubbins had come out too.

Tiny black shapes darted through the evening sky silhouetted against a full moon. The bats were out. A nip on her arm told her the mosquitoes were out too. She slapped her arm. *You missed one,* she told the darting creatures.

The weariness of the long day and the drive had begun to catch up to her. She yawned and turned to go in. A coyote howled in the distance and Nubbins moved closer to her side and Carrie gave him a pat of reassurance as they went back into the house.

Linda strolled toward her in good humor. It seemed that Scott had promised to take her up to his parents' house the next afternoon and show her the remodeling project. Bidding them all a good night, she went upstairs to her room, a pleased smile on her face.

Back in her own room, Carrie imagined the wedding, with her father in a tuxedo escorting her down the long aisle of the big church. She smiled to herself. He hated suits and tight collars. Then her thoughts strayed to thinking of her wedding night. Would it be all she imagined? She remembered again the scene in her apartment and Andrew wanting to make love to her. His response when she backed away. She turned out the light and lay wearily back against the pillow, staring into the darkness.

CHAPTER TEN

*L*INDA DROVE WITH a heavy foot on the accelerator and as the big car roared along the highway, Carrie began to wish she'd driven her own. She'd offered, but Linda had her own way as usual. As it turned out, the beautiful Lexus belonged to Linda's boss because her own car was in the shop. It crossed Carrie's mind to wonder why any boss would loan such an expensive car to an employee, but as it wasn't her business, she left it alone. Glancing at her cousin out of the corner of her eye, she asked casually,

"So, who's the man of the moment, Linda?" It was meant to be teasing, but Linda's face took on a hard look.

"I haven't found Prince Charming and His Daddy Warbucks, if that's what you mean." She shook her head. "Of all the guys I've known, they all want a lot more than they're willing to give." There was a note of bitterness.

This sudden revelation startled Carrie. There had always been boys buzzing around Linda. She went on lots of dates, but as Carrie recalled, there was never one special boy for any length of time.

"I've always envied you, Linda. You seemed to have it all and I was so shy in high school. I always wished I could be more outgoing like you."

"Funny isn't it," Linda mused, "I was the belle of the ball, so to speak, and you were the wallflower. Looks like you're the one who grabbed the brass ring."

Carrie couldn't think of anything to say and they fell silent for the next few miles into town.

There was an older drug store in Weaverville that carried gift items. Weaverville was a small historic town about 17 miles away from Lewiston. To Carrie, who had gotten used to the convenience and close proximity of shops in the city, it seemed like a long trip to the store. She checked over their list and hoped they would find invitations for the shower as well as the other things on the long list her mother and Linda had put together.

"How did you happen to meet the scion of the antique business?" Linda asked, her left elbow on the armrest and one hand on the wheel. The speedometer was pushing seventy.

With an eye on the speedometer, Carrie told her about her friend Tori and the meeting in the café. Linda listened almost wistfully as Carrie told of the engagement party and meeting Andrew's friends.

Linda clucked her tongue. "He certainly moved fast. Of course you had some intimate dinners and…?"

Carrie ignored the implication. "We really didn't have much time. There were so many people Andrew wanted me to meet. Of course his father wanted me to meet other people he knew."

Linda persisted. "Well, I hope you two at least got to spend some cozy time together." Her glance was knowing and sly.

Carrie blushed. "Of course we did." She refused to elaborate. She knew what Linda wanted to know and while she didn't mind confiding the truth to her mother, she didn't want Linda to think her unsophisticated. She just smiled knowingly. Guilt left a hollow feeling in the pit of her stomach.

They found the drug store. The outside appearance of the building hadn't changed in fifty or sixty years, but the display windows at least looked more inviting than Carrie remembered. Inside, she was pleasantly surprised by the number of interesting gift items. A large display case held cards, wrapping paper, ribbon… and shower invitations.

"These are pretty." Carrie reached for the ones she liked.

"Now cousin, you aren't giving the shower, I am," Linda admonished firmly.

She selected a more modern design.

Stifling a touch of annoyance, Carrie realized that nothing had changed between them. Linda always got her way. But what did it matter? She gave in as she always did with Linda. Smiling sweetly, she pretended indifference and turned to look at another card display that said, "To My Sweetheart."

Andrew called later that morning. "I won't be able to make it this coming weekend, Carrie, a few business problems. The best I can do is Friday, June fifteenth." That was the day before the shower, nearly too weeks away. She tried to hide her disappointment.

"How long will you be able to stay?"

"Probably only the weekend, I'll need to get back before Monday."

"Oh, well I'm sure you'll do the best you can. Everyone is anxious to meet you." She longed for him to say something romantic, something intimate.

It sounded like he said, "I'll bet." Then he spoke quickly, "I mean, that's great. I'll see you then. Sometime late afternoon, okay?" He sounded preoccupied. "Bye for now, babe." And he hung up.

Aware that Linda could hear, she lowered her voice. "That will be fine, darling," she said into the hum of the dial tone. "I understand. I can't wait to see you. I love you too."

At least Andrew would be there for the shower and their friends and neighbors could still meet him.

When they started for home, Linda rolled up the window and put on the air conditioning. The sky was still cloudless and the heat lay like a weight over the whole community. Summer had come early to the mountains and the newspaper promised record temperatures for mid-June. Carrie hoped the meadows wouldn't look too dry.

She wanted Andrew to see the beauty of her mountains.

As they came down the driveway, they passed Scott using a weed-eater to take down the grass around the house. He was making himself useful in exchange for his keep. He wore an old white T-shirt and a pair of cut-off shorts. The hair on his arms and legs was wet with perspiration from working in the hot sun.

"Now that is a delicious sight," Linda purred and waved as they went by.

"This afternoon, Scott?" she called out. Scott acknowledged her with a thumbs-up sign, but looked directly at Carrie.

Lunch was a hurried affair. Her mother had things she wanted to do. Linda went to freshen up and left Carrie to clean up the kitchen.

Around one o'clock Scott came to collect Linda as promised for the trip up the hill.

"Do come. It should be interesting." Linda smiled sweetly at Carrie for Scott's benefit, but her eyes signaled "back off." Which she did, willingly, telling Scott she just had a million things to do.

Scott lifted his eyebrows but said nothing. She watched them drive off with Linda chattering away, and tried to ignore the unsettled feeling she had. She didn't really want to go—or did she?

The house was quiet and Carrie decided to go in search of her mother.

Helen was in the garden eyeing a drooping tomato plant. There were over a dozen plants, each loaded with ripening fruit.

"Hi, Mom. Just wondered what you were doing."

"Just getting these tomato plants tied up. We're having a bumper crop this year. I hope everyone doesn't get tired of tomatoes."

Carrie sat down on an old stump and watched her mother deftly arrange the overburdened vine and bind it to the trellis.

Helen looked over her shoulder. "You look pretty serious for a girl about to get married." She came over and looked down at Carrie. "Let's go sit down by the water. It's a lot cooler there."

They went down to a big white bench that sat in the grass at the edge of the river Feeling the perspiration run down her back, Carrie was tempted to jump in the cool water.

Helen waited for Carrie to unburden herself.

"Mother, I know Daddy's concerned about the fact that Andrew isn't a Christian yet, but it's just going to take some time."

Helen looked out across the river. "That's a serious concern, honey. You're a grown woman now and you need to make your own decisions. It will help your father and me to meet Andrew."

They sat quietly for a long time, staring out at the river, each with her own thoughts. The river made a soft, hushing sound as it flowed by. Looking up toward the mountains, Carrie noticed that the peaks still had a trace of snow. It seemed strange to look at snow when the temperature was over a hundred and ten in the shade.

Finally Helen stood up. "I better see about dinner. Want to help?"

"Sure."

They hugged and headed back to the house. She sighed, for there were things Carrie wanted to talk about, but how could she voice them before they met Andrew? She had to give him a chance to impress her parents.

CHAPTER ELEVEN

SUNDAY MORNING AS Carrie and Linda were welcomed and embraced by friends, Linda made it a point to nonchalantly call attention to Carrie's ring. It confirmed Linda's reason for going to church.

And what are your reasons, Carrie? The thought came unbidden and she sank down in the pew as if the words had been said aloud.

The sermon was about laying hold of God's promises. Not the ones we choose to claim from the Bible, but the promises God has spoken to our hearts from His Word. Carrie glanced over at the well-worn hands of her mother as she sat next to Mike, content with her life. Carrie pursed her lips. Why couldn't everyone be happy for her and her coming marriage? Was it so important that Andrew share her faith? Yet, even as she asked the question, she knew the answer.

Sensing her mother's glance, she looked toward the pulpit, for all intents and purposes absorbed in the sermon.

After the service, Pastor Richards shook her hand as they went out. "It's good to see you again, Carrie. I hear there is a wedding in the works. Just let me know the date. We'll be glad to make arrangements for you."

She was obliged to again explain that the wedding would take place at the church in La Jolla. Pastor Richards still smiled. "Oh. Well, I'm sure that will work out better for you both." To her relief she senses no recriminations or hint of disappointment.

As soon as lunch was over, Linda went upstairs to gather her things to return to the city. It was a long, five-hour drive and she wanted to get there before dark.

"After all, I'm a working girl. I have to earn my living, not like some people I could mention." It was said lightly, in a teasing way, but there was a touch of envy in her tone.

"I'll let you know if I can come early Thursday before the shower."

She gave them all brief hugs and got into the sleek Lexus.

"Drive carefully, dear." Helen stood back. She hated goodbye scenes.

"Guess I'd better, for the boss's sake," Linda laughed, and with a wave of her well-manicured hand and a flash of bracelets, she was off.

They watched the car move up the driveway and out of sight down the road, then collectively winced as the loud rattling of the boards on the bridge told them Linda wasn't adhering to the posted five miles per hour. Mike shook his head and they turned back toward the house. Carrie's father headed for his woodshop to work on some birdhouses he was making to tack on trees along the river.

Carrie absorbed herself in a book for the afternoon, feeling guilty to be so relieved that Linda was gone. Her mother fanned herself and declared they were having a shrimp salad for dinner. It was too hot to think of anything complex.

Around five o'clock, Carrie automatically began setting the oak table in the kitchen. It would be just the three of them, for Scott had let them know he was eating dinner with his folks.

Mike said grace, very much like Scott's. Carrie bowed her head and shook off the heaviness that weighed on her spirit. She had everything to be thankful for, a handsome fiancé who loved her. He did, didn't he? A wonderful future, but the thought persisted. *Is this the future I truly want?*

If her parents noticed her preoccupation during dinner, they didn't comment on it. Once she glanced over and her eyes met her mother's. What did she see there? Compassion? Concern? Pity? It was a relief when the meal was over and each of them turned to their own pursuits.

Walking around the living room, she scanned the bookshelves. Her family had a weakness for books and frequently added to their library from various secondhand shops or garage sales. Carrie wondered just how horrified her future father-in-law would be if he realized how much they all loved garage sales. She doubted that there was anything secondhand in the Van Zant home, unless of course it was an antique. But then, perhaps collectors didn't think of antiques as secondhand. They were only expensive treasures to accumulate.

She settled in the old armchair with a good book, relieved she was not rushing to some social affair fretting that she wasn't dressed properly for the occasion. Then, with a start Carrie realized the direction her thoughts were taking. There would be many more social occasions to face when she married Andrew. She concentrated on her book.

The next few days passed in quiet routine. With the extreme heat there was extra watering to do and her mother enlisted her help with the garden. After having to take such care of her appearance these past two months Carrie found that weeding in the garden was almost therapeutic. Due to her mother's efforts, many jars of shimmering red beets, green beans, tomato sauce, and marinara sauce would fill the shelves of their storage room this fall. The zucchini that was to go into cookies or cakes was grated and then quick frozen.

In between chores, she read, talked on the phone with high school friends, and chatted with neighbors when she got the mail at the post office. Her four bridesmaids had been apprised that their dresses were in and they'd been mailed directions to the church.

She helped one day behind the counter at the bookshop and enjoyed herself as she had before college, serving desserts, and making espresso and lattes for customers.

In her free time she sorted out things in her bedroom at home, dawdling over what to take and what to leave behind, recalling memories behind every treasure. She touched the smooth surface of a seashell she'd found on a trip to the coast with the youth group. Then she contemplated a small blue vase she'd bought at a garage sale for twenty-five cents and happily carted home. It held a single pink silk rose. But each time she tried to picture a treasure in the home she and Andrew would share she reluctantly returned the item to the shelf or drawer, sure that it would seem out of place amid the opulence of the Van Zant home. Sometimes, uncomfortable with making decisions, she took herself off for a walk.

One afternoon, down by the river, Carrie finally allowed herself to contemplate Scott Spencer. He hadn't been to dinner all that week. He was helping with some work on his parent's house and evidently was eating most of his meals with them. Was he avoiding her? And why was he still unmarried? She couldn't imagine why one of the adoring girls at his church had not snatched him up. Commenting on this at lunch that day she found herself with mixed emotions when her mother breezily mentioned he was seeing a girl in Weaverville.

Today, as she watched the river flow by with its soothing swishing and hushing sounds, she decided not to think about Scott any more. After all, what was he to her? She leaned back in the warmth and, shaded by a cottonwood, nodded off.

...she was floating down the river in a boat of some kind...listless... her hand trailing in the water. It was too heavy to lift. Someone was calling her name...didn't want to listen...just drift down the river. Sounds of rushing water...danger...trying to turn her head...couldn't move. Someone calling her name over and over, trying to help her... taking her hand...

Waking with a start, she found Nubbins nudging her hand with his soft muzzle. It was only a dream. She smiled at him and stroked his silky ears. Then her name was called again. It was her mother.

"I think I better get moving, Nubbins. It sounds serious. Did she send you to fetch me?" Nubbins wagged his tail and happily trotted at her side as she hurried back up the path to the house.

"Carrie, I've looked everywhere for you," her mother said. "Scott called. His church is having a big potluck dinner and they're hosting a group that travels to various churches putting on plays. He says he heard they are really good and asked us to come. Your father and I think we'll go. You're welcome to come too."

She shrugged. "I guess that will be all right. I like plays. When is it?"

"Well that's why I was trying to find you. It's this evening. The potluck is at six and the program is at seven. It's four-thirty now so we have to hurry. I tossed a salad and put a casserole from the freezer into the oven to bake."

Her practical mother, who had only to pull a carefully prepared casserole from the freezer for an emergency. Carrie thought of the lavish dinners at the Van Zants' with a full-time cook to prepare gourmet meals for father and son. No homemade casseroles from the freezer. For a moment Carrie thought of what it would be like to have all her meals prepared and served to her. No helping with canning or setting the table or baking cookies. The cook would probably not appreciate having someone in her kitchen. Carrie would be in the way. Oh well, she would get used to it, she supposed. She turned to face her mother.

"What can I do to help?"

As they were rushing around getting ready, it occurred to Carrie to ask why they had been invited at the last minute. "The least Scott could do is give us a little notice."

Helen ignored the petulant tone. "His mother just reminded him of it. He has been working so hard on the house with the contractor. You know men. They don't keep track of things like this.

Carrie put the familiar items in the picnic basket. "Is Dad coming?"

"He has a meeting. He'll join us at the church."

Nola Spencer met Carrie and her mother when they walked in the door of the church. She smiled broadly.

"Carrie, we're so glad you could come. I'm sorry I haven't been down since you got home. We have been up to our ears with the work on the house. One problem after another."

Nola was a tall woman, with silvered hair that swept back from her temples like wings. Her face was creased from many smiles and she gestured a lot with her hands, her long tapered fingers emphasizing her words. Carrie felt her warmth and responded with a smile.

"I hope to get up to see the remodeling soon, Mrs. Spencer. I wasn't able to make it the day Linda was there."

"Oh don't you worry about that. We'll see you when you have time. I know you are getting ready for the wedding. I'm looking forward to meeting Andrew at your shower."

"That's great." Carrie hadn't even looked at the guest list to see who had responded. "It's nice of you to come. I'm looking forward to having Andrew meet my family and friends."

A man cleared his throat and Nola turned to the tall, portly gentleman next to her. His black beard and mustache were streaked with gray. Carrie thought that if they were white he would make a great Santa Claus.

"Oh, now where are my manners. Allen, do you remember Carrie—Helen Dickson's girl?"

"Of course, woman. We've lived together in the same neighbor-hood for years."

There was a twinkle in his eyes. Carrie hadn't seen much of Allen Spencer through the years, but she remembered that she always liked him very much.

"Allen! Behave yourself." Nola looked fondly at her husband. "You'd think after thirty-five years I'd have him tamed, but it's a losing battle."

Just then, Mike Dickson hurried in to join them. He was a man who loved to eat, and potlucks were something he seldom missed unless a fire was brewing somewhere. The men shook hands and clapped each other on the back.

Helen deposited the casserole and salad on the designated tables.

Allan looked around. "Let's stop holding up traffic here. Maybe the Dicksons would like to share our table, Nola."

"Wonderful idea. We have plenty of room."

Her father and Allan chatted amiably as Nola led the way to a table that was right in front of the stage.

"We always like to be able to see and hear the performances." The last Nola directed at her husband and Carrie noticed for the first time that Allen Spencer wore hearing aids in both ears. Not wanting to hurt anyone's feelings, she said nothing. She would have liked a less conspicuous location.

Scott and a rather petite girl joined them. She was pretty in an elfin way, with large brown eyes and short auburn hair cut just at her jaw line. She reminded Carrie of a deer. The girl looked adoringly at Scott. When she saw Carrie her eyes held a question.

"Margo, these are our neighbors, Mike Dickson, his wife, Helen, and their daughter, Carrie. Carrie is home preparing for her wedding in July. Ladies, this is Margo Cane."

At the mention of the wedding, Margo showed visible relief and put out a friendly hand to Carrie.

"It's so nice to meet you all," she murmured in a soft, whispery voice. "Scott has just been telling me how kind you are to give him a place to stay while his parents remodel their house." The hand returned to rest possessively on Scott's arm.

They found places at the table and bowed their heads while the pastor of the church said a blessing over the food. When their table number was called and they got in line with their plates, Carrie found Margo at her elbow.

"I just love potlucks, don't you? I love to cook. I made a chocolate cake. Scott loves my chocolate cake."

Carrie smiled politely. So, this was the type of girl who appealed to Scott Spencer. Maybe she just didn't know Scott very well. In any case, it shouldn't matter to her at all.

Margo persisted. "Scott says you're neighbors. How close do you live?"

"We're at the bottom of the hill, by the river. Have you known Scott long?"

"Since Sunday school. Quite a few years. He is so sweet, and it means so much to me that he really loves our Lord."

Carrie resisted rolling her eyes. "Yes, of course, I'm sure it does." She smiled sweetly at Margo and continued. "Are you, ah, engaged or something?" she asked innocently.

Margo blushed modestly. "Not yet."

I'm sure you'd like to be, along with half the girls in this church, Carrie mused. Out loud she said, "I wish you well. Scott is a nice person. He's been a great help to my folks."

"Isn't that just like him," Margo gushed, "always thinking of other people."

Scott was standing a few feet back, talking to his father. He looked up and caught Carrie's eye. She could have sworn she saw a slight smile cross his face before he turned back and resumed his conversation. Helen was talking cabbages and corn with a woman next to her and her father was discussing the coming art festival in Weaverville with Allan. Carrie reluctantly turned her attention back to Margo, who was still talking…

"…so you are getting married in July? Is your fiancé from around here?"

"No, he's from San Diego."

About that time Margo got a glimpse of Carrie's engagement ring. Her eyes opened wide in astonishment. "That's a beautiful ring, just beautiful. What does your fiancé do?" She had taken Carrie's hand to get a closer look at the diamond.

Carrie withdrew her hand gently. "His father owns an import company. European antiques. Andrew works for him."

"European antiques, imagine that. My, you really are so fortunate. I pray the Lord will really bless your marriage. I feel fortunate too. I've admired Scott from afar for so long. Well, when one is really happy, they just want everyone around them to be happy too. Don't you think?"

Obviously Margo had taken possession.

Carrie finished filling her plate. "I'm sure that's true. Maybe I'll be hearing of your own wedding soon."

Another modest blush from Margo. Carrie grimly kept a smile on her face and headed for their table, making an unobtrusive shift in seats so she sat between her mother and Nola Spencer. Her mother ended up sitting next to Margo. No one seemed to notice as the others took their seats, except Scott. Seating Margo, he glanced at Carrie, but his expression was bland.

Just after most of them had finished dessert, there was a fanfare of music from the tape deck hidden behind the curtain and a young man stepped to the microphone.

"Folks, we need to start our program. Hope you have all gotten enough to eat."

There were groans from the audience. "Well, that's great. Let's give a rousing Pine Chapel thanks to all the ladies who honored us by making all this fine food." Everyone applauded enthusiastically.

"Now let us bow our heads and give thanks for the program we are about to enjoy. May it touch every heart in this room."

He prayed and then introduced the group as the lights dimmed. The play depicted a modest Jewish family in the days following the death of Jesus. Obviously, they were believers and feared the persecution that had begun for those who followed the forbidden sect know as "The Way." It was a moving performance, and in the end, as the son of the family was dragged off by Roman soldiers, Carrie felt like weeping. Then the little family got on their knees and began to pray, not only for their son who was taken, but for the Roman soldiers. Carrie felt outrage that they would pray for such men. How could God allow such suffering? She became caught up in the play, as though she were there in that home, two thousand years before. The face of the father, mother, and sister radiated such joy.

"We shall see our Aaron," the father intoned, "he shall be waiting for us when our time comes. Be comforted, mother. Be comforted, my Rachel, we shall see our son and brother again. Our Lord has promised it shall be so."

A picture suddenly came to Carrie's mind out of the past. She was very young and was sitting on her mother's lap. Granny Dickson was reading her a story and Carrie remembered her speaking those words: "Our Lord has promised it shall be so—".

Tears threatened to well up in her eyes and she fought them back. She didn't know why she felt like crying. It must have been the emotion of the play. She glanced up to see Scott watching her, and wondered momentarily why. Then she looked away to join the others in a round of applause as the minister took the stage.

"I'm sure we have all been touched to our core by this wonderful play depicting the trials that faced the faithful who followed Christ so many years ago. I know that there are those among us today who are facing trials and a testing of their faith. Our Lord said that when we are weak, then He is strong. He will never give us more than we can bear. He gave us the gift of the Holy Spirit to strengthen and encourage us, and He gave us His Word to guide our way. A wise man once said "If you don't know what to do, do what you know to do." When you don't know the way, get into His Word. He'll show you the way. He has a plan for your life and His plans are for our good, not evil. If you haven't trusted in His care and given your life to Him as Lord and Savior, won't you do so now? I'm going to pray a prayer and I'm inviting each one of you to pray that prayer with me. Say it if you know the Lord, but especially, say it if you do not. It will change your life."

As the pastor led them through the prayer, Carrie dutifully prayed out loud with everyone else at their table. As they finished, she felt a great longing well-up in her for something she couldn't name or describe. She wanted to get away by herself and think.

The pastor asked if anyone would like to stand to publicly acknowledge the decision they had made. Five people stood hesitantly. People crowded around them, smiling, hugging them, and praising God. All Carrie wanted to do was leave, as quickly as possible.

Helen gathered their things, and as they all said goodbye to Scott and his parents, thanking them for sharing their table, Carrie gave a brief smile and nod to Margo. She wondered what Linda's reaction would have been to Scott's choice.

As they moved toward the door with the crowd, someone touched Carrie's arm.

It was Scott.

"I'm glad you came. Are you all right?"

Why did he always see what she didn't want him to see? "It was a good play. Yes, I'm fine. Just a little tired, I guess. I'm usually touched by a good drama." She couldn't look at him for she felt she was going to cry again.

"God loves you, Carrie. Remember that."

She nodded. Why did Scott have to say that? She stepped out into the humid air, struggling with her emotions. When she felt she had them under control, she looked up but Scott was gone.

CHAPTER TWELVE

*M*ONDAY MORNING DAWNED bright and clear. Watching the sun stream through the window, Carrie looked around at all her familiar things. She thought of her little apartment in the city and chewed on her lower lip. Andrew had wanted her to clear it out as soon as possible.

"Oh Andrew, I just need a little time to sort things and make arrangements for them."

Andrew looked around her apartment as though it was a pile of old clothes they were discussing. The wave of his hand encompassed all that she'd possessed in the last four years.

"Why don't you just call one of those charity trucks? They can take the whole lot away without any trouble." He put his arm around her reassuringly. "You don't need any of it anyway, Darling."

Her family had always been savers and keepers. She pictured two burly men tossing her things in the back of a truck. An idea dawned. She would have everything sent to her home. Her mother would understand and make a place for them.

She took a deep breath and flung back the covers. Feeling immensely better, she pulled on her robe and went to the window to look out at the river.

Little flecks of gold glittered on the water and the scrub jays were loudly squawking at one another. Down on the trail by the river, a doe stepped cautiously, looking around as she placed each dainty foot. Behind her came two very small spotted fawns. Carrie stood very still, because she knew the doe would be alert to any movement—even from the second story of the house. She watched the little family move along, nibbling on the grass. Then, trying to suppress a yawn, Carrie automatically covered her mouth with her hand, a movement not missed by the doe. She hurried her two fawns into the trees, out of sight. Carrie knew they would be safe in the woods. The valley was posted, so no hunting was allowed and deer were a common sight. After living in the city for the last few years, Carrie realized she had missed seeing them.

Though the day was just beginning, the air was already warm with no sign of a breeze. The thermometer on the porch had read over a hundred for the last several days, and that was in the shade. Today promised to be another day of oppressive heat.

There were sounds from downstairs, doors opening and closing and the murmur of voices. Carrie straightened her bed and quickly washed her face. Slipping into a pair of denim shorts and a pink T-shirt, she tied her hair back with a ribbon, pushed her feet into some sandals, and hurried downstairs.

Scott was standing in the entry talking earnestly to her father and mother. They looked up as she came down the stairs. Scott's eyes lingered on her face briefly.

"What's going on? Everyone looks very serious this morning." She looked from one to the other.

"I was just telling your folks that we are concerned about how dry everything is on the mountain. The debris is like tinder. There is a logging crew up there working and all it would take is one spark to set things off. We're keeping an eye on them, but we can't stop them from working."

"You're worried about a fire?" Helen was matter-of-fact.

"I guess anyone would be under these conditions. It just pays to be careful. Our house is closest to the base of the mountain." He grinned. "Sure would hate to lose all that hard work!"

Making light of the danger, they all laughed, but the warning was there.

Scott shrugged. "I guess there is nothing we can do except be watchful, and pray."

"Prayer is the best protection," her father agreed, "the second best is a fire system."

Scott turned to him with sudden interest. "A fire system?"

"Regulation fire hoses and nozzles. And a gas powered generator to pump water from the river. Fire can cut off electricity, you know. Come on, I'll show it to you."

Carrie was curious and followed them outside. Her mother had mentioned something about it in a letter, but she'd had other things on her mind at the time and hadn't paid much attention.

Down by the river there was a small structure like a doghouse. Mike lifted the roof off to expose the generator. Scott examined the mechanism and Mike demonstrated how it started. The sputter of the motor seemed loud in the still air. He turned it off with a nod of satisfaction.

Scott pursed his lips. "Good motor. Where are the lines?"

Mike pointed along the ground in both directions from the motor. "They run about six inches under the ground from the pump around both sides of the house. Those boxes on the trees hold the hoses."

Scott rubbed his chin. "Looks like a good idea. At least you're close enough to the river to use this. My folks would have to run a pipe clear down the hill with easements through several other properties, including yours, to get to the river to do anything like this. All we have are the garden hoses. We could pump from the well, but that takes electricity and the pressure wouldn't hold up under a long period of heavy use." He turned to Mike. "I guess it takes a man from the Forestry Department to be really prepared."

Mike beamed. Carrie felt a sense of pride that her parents had done such a practical thing.

Scott turned to Carrie. "I'm taking the mountain road up to Brown's Mountain to pick up something at the ranger station. There's a lookout up there with a great view. Care to come along?"

Caught unawares, she hesitated, but found that the idea appealed to her. It might be her last chance in a long time to go up to the mountain.

"That would be nice. Yes, I'd like to go. When do I have to be ready?"

"Why don't you have breakfast, and I'll be back to pick you up in about half an hour."

"All right."

Scott seemed pleased, and with a wave of his hand headed out the door.

Helen watched him go. "Such a nice young man, that Scott." She smiled at Carrie. "It will be good for you to get out a bit. You'll be able to see for miles on a day like this." She turned toward the house but glanced back.

"Now you just come into the kitchen and let me get some breakfast into you. You're looking a bit thin these days."

"Just toast and coffee, mother, I'm not too hungry this morning. Maybe it's just too hot."

"Carrie Dickson, that's no proper breakfast. How about a bowl of my special granola with a fresh peach cut up on top? And a small glass of orange juice?

Carrie wrinkled her nose. She knew it wouldn't do any good to argue. She got the orange juice out of the refrigerator and poured a glass. The peach was delicious, as was the granola, and she did feel better. As it turned out, she didn't even want the coffee. She made a mental note to eat better breakfasts, and then wondered what kind of breakfasts the Van Zants ate. Maybe she could yet persuade Andrew to buy a house of their own. She imagined herself fixing his coffee every morning and scrambling eggs.

"Don't know what you're daydreaming about, but you'd better change your shoes. Sandals won't do for walking around pine needles."

Carrie came back to reality with a start. Putting her dishes in the sink, she hurried upstairs to change into her tennis shoes.

She had mixed emotions about going with Scott this morning. Why hadn't he invited Margo? Maybe he didn't have enough time. It was a long round trip into Weaverville to pick her up. Considering their tenuous relationship this last week, she wondered. *Why did he invite me?* She turned back to tying her shoelaces.

Scott drove his dad's Blazer with four wheel drive, which was the perfect vehicle for a run up the mountain.

Helen hurried out of the kitchen as they stood at the front door. "Here, I packed a picnic lunch. There aren't going to be any snack shops where you young folks are going." She handed them the picnic basket and Scott beamed.

"Mrs. Dickson, you sure know how to get to a man's heart. If you weren't married to Mike, I'd marry you myself and insure all these good meals."

Her mother waved a hand impatiently. "Scott Spencer, you stop trying to flatter me. Now you two get out of here before I take my basket back." She made shooing motions at them and then stood on the porch as they laughingly got in the car and drove away.

Now, alone with Scott, Carrie felt like she was back in high school and just as tongue-tied. They rode along in silence for a few minutes until Scott finally spoke.

"I don't bite, you know. I've been known to make perfectly innocent conversation and hardly ever attack young damsels I make off with in my trusty Chevy." He looked straight ahead but a smile was tugging at the corners of his mouth.

Carrie giggled and began to relax. She shook her head and looked out the window. "You always made me feel tongue-tied. You were the big football hero and I always felt overwhelmed when you gave me a lift to school. How you stood me I don't know."

The smile was more somber. "You were a nice girl, Carrie, always living in Linda's shadow. Maybe you didn't realize how pretty you were, and are."

"That's a nice thing to say, Scott."

"I wanted to talk to you, but you always hurried away like a scared rabbit. Guess I kind of gave up. Then, before I knew it you went off to college and were hardly ever home."

Carrie nodded. "Now here we are, both college graduates. You a teacher, and me, well, engaged to be married."

Scott's hands tightened on the wheel. He was silent for a moment and then asked casually, "So, tell me about Andrew. He must be a pretty special guy."

Carrie rambled on, telling him how they met, about the parties and the people she'd been introduced to. She told him of the wonderful places Andrew had taken her to.

"You should see the mansion they live in, Scott. I'm not sure I'm comfortable with that yet, someone to cook all the meals, a staff to clean up everything. I'm going to fulfill my teaching contract for a year, but after that I'm not sure what I will find to do, but there are organizations that need volunteers.

"Charity work. Well, that is a worthy occupation."

She looked closely at him to see if he was teasing her, but his expression remained bland.

He didn't comment much as she talked, but listened quietly as the Chevy made its way up the grade to the top of the mountain range.

The ranger station came into view presently. As they pulled up front, a man came out to meet them. "Scott, good to see you, how are things going?" He glanced at Carrie and raised his eyebrows. "Nice company."

"Now don't go getting ideas. She's just a friend from the neighborhood. Thought she'd enjoy a last trip up the mountain before she marries a city boy in July. Carrie, meet Rob Wheeler."

She put out her hand. "It's nice to meet you, Rob."

"Same here. Say, Scott, how'd you let some city guy get away with the best looking girl I've seen in these parts?"

Scott shook a fist playfully. "Okay, buddy, cut it out." He turned to Carrie.

"Rob and I were roommates in college. He still thinks he can get away with murder."

The men clapped each other on the back and headed into the ranger station with Carrie following behind.

Rob picked up a packet. "Here's the map of the mountain behind your house with all the old lumber roads marked, like you asked for. I included a map of Brown's Mountain just for good measure.

Normally, it would be at the ranger station in town, but I brought it here to check it over after you called."

The two men pored over the map, talking quietly. Left to herself, Carrie looked around. An old pair of snowshoes hung on the wall and the condition of the leather showed they were more for decoration than practical use. There were large maps on the wall and various stacks of books and pamphlets. A desk was piled with a motley accumulation of paperwork. She guessed a couple of month's worth. Maybe this station wasn't used that often. The head of a buck hung on the wall. He had a fine rack of antlers. She looked at him with regret. It seemed a shame to kill a beautiful animal like that. Her family had always hated September when deer season started. Hunters' trucks were parked at the head of every access road in the county and even though their valley was off limits to deer hunters, the sound of gunshots could be heard on the nearby mountain. Hunters ignored the no-trespassing and no-hunting signs that were posted and came across the bridge into their private area of homes. It was only through the perseverance of the residents that they were caught and sent out of the area. Still they found ways. A beautiful buck had been found wandering down their road with an arrow through its neck. Somehow it had survived.

There was another trophy on the wall and she looked at it curiously. She didn't recognize the animal at all. It had a soft nose and large eyes and a small set of antlers, like an antelope, only smaller. As she puzzled over what it was, a voice spoke behind her and she jumped.

"Rare critter. A jackalope. Hardly see one around these days. That one may be the last of its kind," Rob intoned solemnly.

"How could anyone kill an animal that is the last of its kind? Someone should have taken the trouble to save it." She turned around indignantly only to find the two men barely suppressing their laughter. Bewildered, she looked from one to the other, "Am I missing something?"

They guffawed, slapping each other on the back. "Hey, Scott, I think we got us another tenderfoot here."

Scott chewed his lip and tried to look serious. "Yep, I think she needs to be initiated into the Special Order of Jackalopes."

Carrie, hands on her hips, fixed the two men with her sternest look. "What is going on? I think you better let me in on the joke."

Scott and Rob looked at each other in mock seriousness. "What do you think? Guess we'd better 'fess up' Scott. She's liable to throw something at us."

Putting an arm around her shoulder, which was unexpectedly disconcerting, Scott turned her back to face the "jackalope."

"Now you have to consider the name, Carrie. Look at the face and head and tell me what the name 'jack' conjures up for you."

She looked closer. Jack. "Jackrabbit?" As soon as she said the word, it suddenly became clear. It was the head of a jackrabbit to which a small pair of antlers was attached. She felt foolish. Well, the joke was on her and she figured she might as well be a good sport. Ten years before, she would have run away in mortification had this situation occurred. Growing up had at least given her courage.

"Okay, the joke's on me." She fixed them with a mischievous grin. "Look out, I may get even."

Both men put up their hands in submission. "Yes ma'am."

She waved a hand at them, dismissing the incident, and shook her head. They were like a couple of overgrown kids.

Rob and Scott shook hands and as they left, Rob winked at her. "Come back anytime, pretty lady."

They headed up one of the fire roads toward the lookout tower.

"Is anyone in the tower now, Scott?"

"Yes. We have volunteers who man the tower for a week at a time. Some stay longer. At some lookout towers volunteers live there all season. Sometimes couples do it together—lots of solitude but plenty to do. There's a bunk and a small cook stove and camp refrigerator. You have to climb down to the ground to pump water from the well."

"Then you've been up there for a week?"

"In past summers, but not this year yet. I'm scheduled for a week in mid-July. I may go back again in late August if they need me."

"Can anyone work the tower?"

"The scanners are pretty carefully selected. They want people who know the mountains and are responsible. We have a short training time. We're told what to look for and how to report what we see. Mostly it means scanning the mountain and surrounding valleys for signs of smoke and determining the location. We call our information in to the ranger station on the radio phone and they check it out."

"It sounds like a really necessary job. I'm looking forward to going up in the tower."

"Luke Early is in the tower this week. George said he would call him on the radio phone and warn him we're coming."

"Does he have to open a gate or anything?"

"Well, no. When working up there you are usually by yourself—some of the guys tend to be pretty, ah, casual."

"Casual?

"Um, no shirts, no shaving, rare showers, just a bag of water hung in the sun to heat for a little washing up."

Carrie got the picture. She imagined the man in the tower hurrying to get a shirt on and pick up a little before they got there.

A tall rail of a man strolled out to meet them. He wore a black hat that had a stained leather band with a feather in it. His jeans looked like they had never seen the inside of a washing machine. His dark eyes contemplated her from under thick, bushy brows. His heavy beard and mustache reminded her of a picture she'd seen at the ranger station of an old miner outside his cabin. From the perspiration stains under the arms of his cotton shirt, she decided that he hadn't felt the need to change it for them. Or, maybe he hadn't brought another shirt.

"Carrie, this is Luke Early, a friend of mine. Carrie's a neighbor, Luke."

"Miss Carrie. Scott." He acknowledged them with a soft, southern drawl.

"Mind if we come up to the tower? I wanted to show Carrie what we do up here."

"All right." Luke appeared to be a man of few words. He saw her glancing at his clothes. "Pardon me, ma'am, been choppin' a little wood."

Carrie expected stairs of some kind, but found herself climbing a ladder that was let down and lifted back up by a pulley system.

Luke began to climb back up and Scott indicated that Carrie go next. He followed her. Once up the ladder, Luke showed Carrie how he pulled the ladder back up.

"Why don't you have stairs?"

"Well, Miss Carrie, the tower is in a pretty remote area. Mountain lion and bear country. It's safer for the spotter if he can pull the ladder up at night. If you notice, there are barriers around the tower itself so no animal can climb up into the tower. Cept' maybe squirrels." Luke Early could talk a bit when he wanted to.

Carrie shuddered. She imagined a scanner sleeping peacefully up in the tower with a huge mountain lion prowling around outside trying to figure a way to get up to him. "Why would a mountain lion bother you? I thought they stayed away from people."

"They smell food," Scott offered, "Also, with the laws protecting them, the mountain lions have become bolder as the years go by—best to take precautions."

"Now Scott," Luke drawled, "we don't want to overdo it." He turned to Carrie. "Most of the time we can leave the ladder down. It's pretty quiet."

Carrie couldn't see the look on Scott's face because he had his back to her. She breathed a little easier though. She had been looking at the trees outside expecting to see a mountain lion appear at any time. Then Luke added, "Had a little company night before last, though. Heard it growlin' low in its throat, you know? Kept my rifle handy."

Carrie looked back at the clearing and the nearby trees. She would feel better when they were safely back in the Blazer and headed down the mountain.

"Carrie. Look over here." Scott took her elbow and steered her to the other side of the lookout. Isn't that an awesome sight?"

She caught her breath. The carpet of trees covered the mountains for as far as she could see like a benevolent blanket. The river wound down among them, a tiny ribbon of gray-blue. There was no sign of life, as the highway wasn't visible. A man would only be a dot on the landscape. The vast sky and craggy peaks of the Trinity Mountains formed a postcard picture.

"It's so beautiful. No wonder you don't mind taking a turn up here. I don't think a person could ever get tired of the view."

"No, don't think anyone could," responded Scott, smiling at her.

"The good Lord did a fine job on all this, I'd say, "Luke murmured.

"Amen, brother," Scott responded softly.

Luke was a believer? Did he go to Scott's church? She didn't recall seeing him there the night of the play. She was sure she wouldn't have missed him. Then she remembered he was probably in the tower.

Once again Scott seemed to pick up on her unspoken thoughts. "Luke and I go back a long time, Carrie. He used to lead my Boy Scout troop when I was about twelve. Taught me all I know about the woods, camping, survival in the mountains—survival in the world. He showed me by his life, and then, he showed me in the Word. He led me to Christ."

Why did Carrie have the feeling this trip up the mountain had more meaning to it? "That was nice of you, Luke," she managed.

Luke glanced briefly at Scott but said nothing. Once, again, she felt the scrutiny of those dark eyes.

The accommodations were as primitive as Scott had described. A simple camp sink, a Primus stove, and a camp refrigerator that was hooked to a small generator. A couple of wooden pegs sufficed for a closet, and the bed looked like it was older than the tower. A bunk with sagging springs. A sleeping bag lay unrolled on it. A table and one chair completed the sparse furnishings. As she looked around, she also realized that there was no bathroom. She was tempted to ask where it was but felt embarrassed.

"Lookin' for something, Miss Carrie?"

"Ah, no. Just seeing what accommodations, I mean, furnishings, you have." She turned to the scenery again to hide her flushed face.

"There's a privy just behind those trees. You can see the edge of the roof."

"Oh, no problem, I'm fine, really. Uh, thanks anyway, Luke." She thought of Luke's reference to the mountain lion a couple of days ago. What if he was still out there somewhere? She'd just get Scott to stop by the ranger station on the way home.

A touch of a smile twitched at the corners of Luke's mouth and he turned back to Scott. "Been quiet, only some fella deciding to burn some trash at the summit. First wisp of smoke and we jumped all over him. Part-timer. Wasn't thinkin' I guess."

"Part-timer?" Carrie looked questioningly at Luke.

"People who just live up in the area part of the year. Like a vacation cabin."

"Oh." She should have figured that out for herself.

Scott stuck his hand out and Luke reached out his gnarly one grabbing Scott in a hug. "Take it easy, little brother."

"We'd better be going, Luke. It's good to see you again. See you at church when you come off your stint up here."

"Sure will. See you there too, Miss Carrie?" Luke was a gentleman in the rough. She almost expected him to tip his hat.

"I don't go to Scott's church, Luke. We live in Lewiston. I go to the Community Church there." It seemed important that she let him know she attended church.

"God's wherever his people are, Miss Carrie. Good you go to church."

"Yes. Well, goodbye, and thank you for letting us come up to the tower. I hope you don't have any more trouble with mountain lions."

Luke chuckled softly and glanced at Scott. "Well, if they won't bother me, I won't bother them."

They climbed back in the Blazer, and as Carrie looked back to wave, Luke tipped his hat.

CHAPTER THIRTEEN

CARRIE REALIZED THEY were taking a different road and would not pass the ranger station. Now what should she do? She was trying to figure out how she would broach the delicate subject when Scott pulled into a primitive campground with a single, small brown building.

"It's not much, but it beats going into the trees."

"How did you know?"

"Saw you looking around a little anxiously. I figured out what you were looking for. After the mountain lion story I didn't think you wanted to venture into the woods by the lookout."

She smiled her thanks.

The door was unlocked because it was still tourist season. There was evidence someone had been here recently, servicing the camp. In the heat, the smell of disinfectant was overwhelming. She was back in the car as soon as possible.

As the Blazer rumbled along, they once again rode in silence, but this time it was more of a companionable silence. Scott was concentrating on negotiating the narrow curves of the road and watching for other vehicles. While they had passed no one, he still honked when there was no way to see if someone was coming from the opposite direction. All at once, an old sedan roared around the next curve nearly meeting them head on. The young man at the wheel jerked the big car to one side, and Scott, uttering one word, "Lord!" skillfully whipped the Blazer to the other side with only inches to spare. Carrie, who had been casually looking at the scenery, was suddenly thrown against the side of the car, her head bumping against the window. Instinctively she covered her face with her arms.

When they came to a stop, she peeked between her arms and found herself looking down at a steep ravine. They were on the edge and she didn't see any land below the Blazer. One lone ancient pine tree grew on the side of the road, and they were up against it.

"You all right?" Scott leaned over and put a hand on her shoulder.

She looked at him, wide-eyed. "I don't know how you avoided him!"

Scott shook his head. "Guess our guardian angels had their work cut out for them." He looked for a long moment at the pine tree. He turned back to Carrie, studying her with concern. "You okay?"

She finally smiled shakily. "I'm okay, really."

Scott got out cautiously and checked their situation. They were still on the road, but just barely. He got back in and started up the car again. Turning the wheel to his left sharply, he closed his eyes for a moment and then stepped on the gas. Carrie knew he was praying. The car lurched onto the road, and they continued on their way.

She looked over at him. "Guardian angels?"

"Sure. You have one, you know."

"I always said that as part of my prayers when I was a little girl. You know, "Now I lay me down to sleep, I pray the Lord my soul to keep. Angels guard me through the night, and wake me with the morning light." She felt a little sheepish having recited a childish prayer.

"I like that prayer. All kidding aside, though, you do have a guardian angel. They don't leave you after you grow up."

"Oh Scott, how do you know that?"

"Matthew, Chapter eighteen, verse ten. Jesus took a little child on his lap and talked to His disciples. He said, "Take heed that you do not despise one of these little ones, for I say to you that in heaven, their angels do always behold the face of My Father.""

"He was talking about children."

"True. But there is no place in the Bible that says those angels are taken away."

She leaned back. The thought of a guardian angel was pleasant. She pictured the angels holding their car on the road and pulling the other car away. Maybe they even made sure that pine tree was there. Rather comforting. "Maybe you're right, Scott. At least I'm glad to have had one today."

Scott laughed and his eyes lingered on her face. This time she didn't look away first.

A fox dashed into the brush by the side of the road and a moment later a jackrabbit crossed in front of them.

She hoped the fox was far enough away so the rabbit was safe. Then she smiled to herself as she remembered the 'jackalope' at the ranger station and wondered how many others had fallen for that joke.

The sun filtered through the pines making interesting patterns on the ground. There were no flowering shrubs and the evidence of the dry summer was everywhere. They passed an old miner's cabin, its ancient logs slowly rotting away with time. There were signs along one portion of the road warning those who passed by to stay on the road. She had heard that you could get shot if you wandered up in these hills and stumbled on a modern-day miner at work.

The other story was that there were people who had marijuana farms up in the hills. The special agents made sure they were well backed-up when they went into these areas. The local paper had run a big article on the pot farms. One setup that agents discovered had three to four thousand plants. The head of the Bureau of Land Management, referred to as the BLM, had said that the growers pleaded they were growing the plants for medicinal purposes according to the law, but the size of the operation had caused the officers to take a dim view of that defense. The huge marijuana farm had been closed down and the plants destroyed.

Carrie tried to look through the trees to see if she could see anything suspicious, but then reasoned that they were probably far from the road.

They began to slow down and Scott turned into an area that had a big flat boulder and plenty of shade. It was on a rise so they had a great view of the valley again. A perfect picnic spot. They got out and Scott hefted the picnic basket and a blanket from the back seat. He handed her a couple of pillows to carry and they set out their lunch.

Carrie's mother had packed a small blue and white tablecloth, some napkins, a thermos of cold lemonade, cups, and forks. There were chicken sandwiches, some leftover coleslaw, carrot sticks, and a dozen chocolate chip cookies Helen had obviously pulled from the freezer. Carrie didn't realize how hungry she was until she saw the food.

She waited patiently while Scott prayed and they tackled the picnic basket.

Later, comfortably full, they propped the pillows against a rock and leaned back. With the warmth of the sun and a full stomach, Carrie could have gone to sleep.

"This is very peaceful. I could look at the mountains forever," Carrie murmured wistfully. She glanced at Scott who had his head back against the rock with his eyes closed. He had such a nice face, a strong chin. *I wonder what it would be like if he kissed me.* Startled by the thought, and feeling like she was somehow betraying Andrew, she looked quickly away and went through the motions of making herself more comfortable. When she looked back at Scott his eyes were open and he was watching her.

"I've told you all about what I have been doing. It's your turn, Scott." She struggled to be casual with those dark eyes studying her.

"What would you like to know about me?" His voice was soft.

"Well, start with what you did after high school."

He straightened up a bit. "Let's see if I can give you a brief summary. I had a football scholarship, as you know, for Humboldt State University, and graduated with a BA in Secondary Education. I heard about an opening at the Christian high school where I teach now and applied for the job. I was hired."

"Do you still spend your summers working in Mexico and places like that?"

His eyebrows went up. "You remember?"

She shrugged. "We all knew that's what you did in the summer when we were in high school. You missed a lot of fun on the lake."

"Maybe we have different interpretations of what is fun, Carrie. I enjoy building things, helping people. There's a certain amount of satisfaction in doing something for someone that they are not able to do for themselves. Also, it's been good experience for me. I can save my folks money by helping with some of the remodeling work. Someday I plan on building my own house."

"When you get married?"

His eyes narrowed a bit as he looked at her. "Yes, probably."

She turned away on the pretext of admiring the view. "I guess that's in the pretty near future."

"Really? Who told you that?"

Now she was uncomfortable again. She looked back at him reluctantly. "I thought you and Margo—" Her voice trailed off, leaving the question hanging.

"Ah, Margo." He looked amused. "She's a nice girl and I have dated her a few times since I've been home, but there is no understanding between us concerning marriage."

At least on your part, Scott Spencer! She folded the napkins carefully. "I'm sorry, I guess I misunderstood. Then, you don't have a special girl in mind at this time?"

"I didn't say that. I said I had no understanding with Margo."

"Oh. Is it a girl down by your school?"

"You're very curious about my love life." Scott grinned at her outrageously.

Now she was defensive. "I don't care who you are dating. It's really none of my business." This was not going well. She suddenly began to gather things together.

Scott reached over and put his hand on hers. "I didn't mean to make you uncomfortable, Carrie."

She felt the strength of his hand and warmth filled her. Taking a deep breath, she leaned back against the rock.

"Are you really happy, Carrie? Is this marriage what you want?"

"Of course I'm happy." She'd responded quickly, too quickly. She turned to him earnestly. "Oh Scott, I'm sure you'll really like Andrew."

"I'm sure I will, if you love him." Scott occupied himself with drawing in the dirt with a stick.

This time she put her hand on his arm. "Scott, I admire your faith. It works for you. You seem so comfortable with God. It comes so natural for you. I don't think I can be like that."

"It doesn't start off that way. It is like getting to know any other friend. You communicate and eventually become closer. When I first found Christ, I was ecstatic, full of joy. I was ready to tackle the world. But I was only twelve and there was a real world out there. Living my faith and dealing with my peers was a pretty hard thing to do. I found I had to stop trying to live it on my own strength and let Jesus live through me."

"I guess I've never really understood how one does that."

"Galatians 2:20 says, 'I am crucified with Christ; nevertheless I live; yet not I but Christ lives in me: and the life I now live in the flesh I live by the faith of the Son of God who loved me, and gave Himself for me.'"

"I still don't understand."

"It means that I don't try to do it myself. I follow Christ and His teachings to the best of my ability and leave the rest to Him. I knew He had a plan for my life, and in time He revealed it to me. I let His Word guide me when I have decisions to make and when there are troubles I can't handle, I give them to the One who can handle them."

"I see." She wasn't sure she did.

"Carrie, have you ever asked Christ into your life?"

She didn't want to answer him. The barrier went up between them again. She looked at the scenery for a long moment. *Had she?*

"Oh, yes. I'm sure I did. In Sunday school I think."

"You don't remember when?"

"How can one remember something that happened a long time ago?" She was stalling and she was sure Scott knew it. She could remember incidents from her childhood, but couldn't remember a time in her life when she actually prayed the words to the sinner's prayer and meant them.

Scott was drawing in the dirt with the stick again. He seemed to be silent a long time. "Maybe we'd better be getting home," he said finally.

Was he upset with her? She began to gather up the picnic things again. Somehow the day had not ended on a positive note and her heart suddenly felt heavy as she stood up.

"Yes, you're right. I have a lot of things to do."

She walked quickly back to the Blazer and at a sound behind her, turned around. Scott was so close that she found herself looking up into his face. His dark eyes seemed to draw her into their depths. He put one hand out on the side of the car and leaned toward her. She knew he was going to kiss her. She wanted him to. Lifting her chin, she closed her eyes and waited. She heard a sharp intake of breath. He took hold of her shoulders with both hands and uttering a soft groan, gave her a brotherly kiss on the forehead.

Her eyes flew open and she felt the blood rush to her cheeks. What was she thinking? She quickly got in the car and stared straight ahead, her eyes filling with tears.

Scott loaded the blanket, pillows, and picnic basket in the back and climbed in. He didn't look at her as he started the engine and headed down the road. They drove in silence for a long time. Finally, Scott pulled over to the side of the road.

"Carrie.

She couldn't look at him. He cupped a hand under her chin and gently turned her head to face him.

"I'm sorry. I did want to kiss you, and not on the forehead. You're beautiful and any man would be crazy not to. But you're engaged, Carrie. It wouldn't have been right. You wouldn't want Andrew going around kissing other women. Maybe all that scenery just got to both of us, okay?"

He seemed so earnest and she nodded her head. He was right. It wouldn't have been fair to Andrew.

"Just remember a nice day with an old friend?"

She responded with a smile in spite of her fragile feelings and they continued on their way.

As they pulled up in front of the house she got out of the car quickly.

Scott put the picnic basket on the porch. "Thanks for going today. It was a nice day, Carrie, in every way."

"I did enjoy seeing the lookout tower and meeting your friends. Thanks for taking me."

"Anytime." Reaching out, he drew a finger down her cheek and she caught her breath. "Andrew is a lucky man," he said softly, and climbed back in the car. In a moment he had driven around the stand of pines at the head of the curved driveway and was out of sight.

No one seemed to be home so Carrie unloaded the picnic basket and stood for a moment listening to the ticking of the old grandfather clock. In three weeks she and Andrew would be married. There was no euphoria. She felt nothing. With a sigh she went slowly upstairs to her room. Her feelings were jumbled and she had to sort them out.

Sitting in the rocking chair, she looked out the window at the river. Scott was right. She was just overcome by the beauty of the mountains. It was a romantic setting. Andrew wouldn't have approved of her going off with Scott like that, would he? Maybe it was best if she just didn't mention this day to him. Needing comfort, she went to the phone and dialed Andrew's number. The housekeeper said he was out of town. That was strange. He hadn't mentioned going out of town. He said he had a lot of work to do. Maybe they had a large shipment come in. If she could just hear his voice and talk to him she knew she would feel much better. It was hard being apart like this. She wanted to feel Andrew's arms around her and have him kiss her. He always made her feel like she was the most beautiful girl in the world.

Carrie looked around the room for something to do, another book, maybe? She could always lose herself in a good story. She wandered over to the bookcase and sat down on the floor, one elbow on her knee and her chin on her knuckles. Her hand moved over a number of titles but finally rested on the Sunday school New Testament. She pulled it out and sat staring at it. She started to put it back and then on impulse, flipped it open. It opened to the Book of Matthew and her eyes fell on a verse:

"And I say unto you, ask, and it shall be given you; seek, and ye shall find; knock and it shall be opened unto you. For everyone that asks receives; and he that seeks shall find; and to him that knocks it shall be opened..."

Was she asking? What was she asking for? The minister and Scott both said God would lead you from His Word. How did He lead you? In the silence of her room, she sat cross-legged on the floor, her Bible in her lap, and continued reading as the afternoon shadows lengthened.

CHAPTER FOURTEEN

CARRIE WOKE TO the sounds of music from downstairs. Good smells wafted up from the kitchen and she stretched lazily. Her hand came down on her Bible and, looking at it, she wondered how long she'd read before she fell asleep. She had looked up several scriptures on the will of God in the concordance in the back of her Bible. In Romans the apostle Paul had said that we were to present our body as a living sacrifice, holy, acceptable unto God, which is our reasonable service; and not to be conformed to this world—but transformed by the renewing of our mind, to prove what was the good and acceptable and perfect will of God.

She turned to a passage in the Book of John: "And this is the will of Him that sent Me, that everyone which sees the Son, and believes on Him, may have everlasting life; and I will raise him up at the last day."

God's will was to believe on His Son. *But I do believe in Jesus.* What more could He ask of her? And how did she go about renewing her mind? She did the best she could and was an intelligent person, a good person. The Bible said not to be conformed to this world. Well, she wasn't a wicked person. Yet, just as she contemplated this thought, a scene flashed in her mind. Was she becoming conformed to Andrew's world? Then the question that she had been pushing to the back of her mind came glaring at her. *Do I want to be conformed to Andrew's world?*

She shook her head. This was silly. Why was she putting herself through all this?

She just needed to see Andrew and everything would be all right. Andrew was coming in just a few days, and this self-examination was a waste of time.

Changing into a pair of long shorts, she freshened herself up and went downstairs. Her parents were talking as they set the table and put the food in place. They stopped when they saw her in the doorway.

"Oh, there you are, darling. I was just about to come and knock on your door. Your dad and I returned from a meeting at the church and didn't realize you were home until we saw the container in the sink. I came upstairs and tapped on your door." Her mother smiled indulgently, "You were asleep on the floor with a pillow under your head. I thought I'd just let you sleep."

"I probably needed the rest. Thanks. Can I do anything?"

"Your timing was perfect," said her dad with a twinkle in his eye, "everything is already done."

They sat down to dinner.

"Did you have a nice day with Scott?" her dad asked casually.

"Yes, I did. I met a friend of his who is a ranger by the name of Rob. They went to college together. Then there was another friend who was in the lookout tower." She looked at them with a mischievous glint in her eye. "Have either of you two ever seen a jackalope?"

Her father burst out laughing. "Don't tell me they had one of those at the ranger station. I saw one once in a sporting goods store."

"They told me it was a rare animal, the last of its kind." She gave a sheepish shrug and joined in the laughter.

"Who was up in the tower?" Helen smiled and buttered a roll.

"His name was Luke Early. He was like a character out of an old western, but very nice."

"Luke. Yes, he is a nice man. From Alabama I believe. He used to be the scoutmaster a few years ago. Now he works for, let me see," She turned to her husband. "Just what does he do now, dear?"

"Works for the Marina, engines and that sort of thing."

"Scott said he was his scoutmaster, and that he led him to Christ." Carrie tossed this into the conversation while moving her potato salad around her plate. She caught a look that passed between her mother and father.

Helen poured a glass of lemonade. "When did he tell you that?"

"When we were in the tower. Oh, by the way, thanks for the picnic lunch, Mom, it was delicious. We ate all of it. Guess getting out in the wilderness is good for the appetite."

"No trouble. I can't have my only daughter up on the mountain without a thing to eat."

Carrie wrinkled her nose at her mother.

Her mother smiled again. "So you came home and took a nap? I can imagine that this heat is getting to all of us. I have about as much energy as a limp dishrag."

Carrie put down her fork. "I read for a while from my Bible. I haven't wanted to for a while, for some reason."

"Was there something you were looking for, Cricket?"

"Well, I was thinking, you know, about what the pastor said on the will of God. I wanted to, I mean, how do you know what God wants you to do? Scott says that it's God's will for him to teach school. How can he be so sure?"

Her mother spoke first. "With me it's a kind of knowing, a sense of peace in my spirit that what I'm doing is the right thing. When I'm going in the wrong direction, I feel a heaviness, a disquieting feeling. You know, when you are apprehensive about something." She turned to her husband. "How would you define it?"

Mike looked thoughtful. "I would say that's as good a description as one can give. It would be nice if God would put a big sign in front of us that tells us which way to go. He sent the Holy Spirit instead, to dwell inside each of us to guide us. Someone who does not know the Lord might say that it is their conscience bothering them. They just have the feeling that something is not right."

Carrie moved some crumbs around on the tablecloth with her finger. "You mean when we go to do something that we know is wrong and we feel uneasy?"

"That's right, dear. Only it's the Holy Spirit within us, telling us to turn away from it."

"Scott asked me if I had ever accepted Christ. That bothered me because I didn't know what to say. He always seemed, well, over-religious. I have always believed I was a Christian, but I cannot remember exactly when I became one." Carrie looked earnestly at her mother. "Why can't I remember?"

Helen reached over and patted her arm. She started to say something and paused, checking herself. Finally, "I'm sure you made that commitment. Why don't you ask the Lord to reveal to you the time and place? He'll show you."

Carrie considered that and nodded thoughtfully. Her mother got up to get more lemonade and put her hand on her daughter's shoulder.

"You'll work it out, honey, just give yourself time."

The words, *and time is running out*, crossed Carrie's mind, but she remained silent. After the dishes were loaded in the dishwasher, they watched the news. Nubbins lay down by Carrie's feet and she patted him absentmindedly.

Mike had returned this morning from fighting another brush fire in the valley. It was caught just in time, but he'd been gone two days, overseeing the crews. The heat was drying out the grass everywhere and people were warned to be extremely careful. So far, the newsman intoned, there were no major fires going and he expressed the hope that they would get through the fire season without that hazard. There were scenes of hills and mountains, all looking extremely dry. Carrie thought of Scott's warning that morning and his mention of the logging crew. The rest of the week was going to carry record temperatures again; in the high 90's and continuing over 100 degrees.

"That weatherman must live around her," muttered Mike, fanning himself with a folded newspaper. They had no air conditioning in the house because it was on the shady side of the river and remained fairly cool most of the day. By evening, though, the house had absorbed enough of the heat to make sleeping difficult, at least until the early morning hours when the outside air was cooler.

Her mother yawned and said she was going to call it a night. Mike got up also. The coyotes set up their familiar chorus across the river and the haunting cries gave Carrie goosebumps. Maybe she should turn on all the outside lights when she went out with Nubbins.

CHAPTER FIFTEEN

ON TUESDAY MORNING Carrie drove into Weaverville, poked around the shops, and bought a turquoise silk blouse. In the drugstore, she picked up a bottle of her favorite cologne and some mascara. Strolling along the sidewalk of the historic town, she felt a little nostalgic. How often would she come back here in the future? Would Andrew want to come here again?

She wandered into an antique shop and saw a small cabinet with delicate hand painting on it. Considering the purchase, she realized that she didn't know where it would go in the Van Zant's home. She didn't even know what their living arrangements would be like. Would they just move into Andrew's room? It was disconcerting to realize that she and Andrew had never talked about it. Would she just arrive with the clothes on her back so to speak, and be shown to their quarters?

She looked longingly at some ruffled curtains and a set of Blue Willow dishes, and wished that they were decorating their own place. That's what most newlyweds did, even if it was a small apartment. Andrew could afford a house. Why did they have to move into the family mansion, like tenants? She shook herself and decided that line of thinking wouldn't do, however, she was going to bring the subject up again when Andrew got here. With a last wistful look at the blue dishes and the little cabinet, she left the shop.

Back in her car, Carrie took the back route to Lewiston on Rush Creek Road. She took her time, looking at the trees and scenery.

Things were so different in the country. In the city she sometimes managed to get to an occasional garage sale on the weekend, running around on residential streets. Here in Weaverville and the surrounding communities, people thought nothing of driving all over the hills and half a mile up a mountain for a yard sale.

On impulse she stopped at a small general store in the historic district that sold everything from fishing lures to antiques with a deli and ice cream parlor thrown in.

"I'll see you Saturday," Mrs. Jorgenson told her gaily as she handed her the cone.

She poked her head in the bookshop and found her mother's part-time worker, Sarah, handling the shop. Sarah handed her a paper plate to put under the cone to save dripping on the floor. They chatted a few minutes but when two customers came in, Carrie slipped out.

At the post office, two women who looked ready to melt sat under an awning at a table with baked goods for sale. They were raising money for the local school house museum.

She got the mail and stamps and stopped to look at the remaining items on their table. An angel food cake, looking a little lopsided with the frosting sliding down the sides of the cake beckoned.

"Real homemade, dear. Not a box mix. It's for a good cause," Mabel Barnes spoke up hopefully.

Carrie bought the cake to the relief of the ladies and wondered how she would get it home without getting frosting on her upholstery. She put it on the floor of the car on top of a newspaper flyer.

"We'll see you Saturday, dear," called Mabel.

It looked as though half the ladies of the community were coming to her shower. Must have been Linda's fancy invitations, or was it curiosity?

When Carrie got home, she handed the gooey cake to her mother who happened to be in the kitchen.

"Bake sale—museum. It's homemade."

Her mother carried the cake to the sink like a dead skunk and stared at it with her hands on her hips. "I'll put it somewhere, but the refrigerator is busting at the seams."

Carrie put the mail on the hall table. There hadn't been any for her. She didn't expect anything from Andrew. He already told her he wasn't very good at writing letters. He preferred the telephone. "And, you aren't very good at that, either," she murmured to herself crossly.

The heat had a definite effect on her temper. Just as she reached the stairs, the telephone rang. Ladies had been calling to respond to the shower invitations. Let her mother answer it, she thought petulantly, and started up the stairs.

"Catch that will you, Carrie? I have my hands full here," Helen called from the kitchen.

Reluctantly she picked up the phone. To her surprise it was Andrew. He sounded distracted.

"Carrie, you'll have to pick me up at the airport Friday. A little, ah, trouble with the car. I just decided to fly over. You and I can drive back in your car, okay?"

No loving preamble...no words that he missed her. Andrew hated flying. What was wrong?

"What happened to your car?"

"Just problems. I'll tell you about it later."

"I'm glad to hear from you, Andrew. I miss you."

"Sorry, I've just had a few things on my mind. I ah, miss you too."

She waited a long moment hoping he would say more along that line. He was silent.

"What time does the plane come in?"

"About three o'clock." He swore vehemently. "I hate those puddle jumpers. Too cramped! Can't be helped. Just pick me up Friday, okay? We may have to leave Saturday evening. I've got things to do."

She winced at the swear words. "But Andrew, you said you were going to spend the weekend. I don't know what time the shower will be over. There will be a lot of people. We'd have to drive back late at night. Couldn't we wait until Sunday afternoon?" She hated the pleading tone in her voice.

There was a heavy sigh on the other end of the phone. He was irritated. "We'll see, Carrie, we'll see."

"Andrew, you aren't getting cold feet are you?" She tried to make it light, teasing.

"Don't worry, Carrie, I'm still planning on the wedding. Don't get all worked up."

Worked up? "Yes, of course. I just… "

"Got to go, I'll see you at the airport, okay? Bye."

"Goodbye, darling."

There was a click. He was gone. Carrie stood staring at the phone in her hand. As she slowly put it on the cradle, a large tear rolled down her cheek. She wiped it away with the back of her hand. Why did she feel like crying? Her lower lip trembled and she hurried upstairs to her room. Putting her face down on her pillow, she began to sob quietly.

Awaking some time later, she felt embarrassed for dissolving into tears. Probably just being a jittery bride. She washed her face and noted that her eyes were not red. At least she wouldn't have to fend off questions from her parents.

Carrie hesitantly crept down the stairs and decided to look for her mother. Helen was in the living room arranging flowers.

"Mother?"

"Hi, honey." Helen glanced up from her project and after noting Carrie's face, gestured toward the couch. "Come sit here and tell me what you have been doing today."

Carrie plunked herself down on the sofa. "Nothing much. I went into town. Bought some things and ran some errands. I got your stamps."

"Thank you, dear." Her mother waited. "Was there something on your mind? You seem a little down."

Carrie had always been able to share things with her mother and yet now she hesitated. She wasn't sure how to start. In fact, she wasn't exactly sure just what was bothering her.

"I feel so, emotional, like I could cry at the drop of a hat. I don't know what's wrong."

"Perhaps you're just a little anxious about the wedding?"

"Maybe. It's just that Andrew called," her voice trailed off.

"He's still coming up here, isn't he?"

"Well, yes. He's not driving though. He said something about car trouble. He wants me to pick him up at the airport Friday afternoon."

"That makes sense if he doesn't have a car."

"Oh, I know. But he hates flying, especially small planes. Some sort of a phobia. He also wants us to leave Saturday night to drive back in my car. He says he has things to do."

"Saturday night? My goodness, Carrie, that's out of the question. You'll be tired, and heaven knows when everyone will leave."

"I told him that. He said, 'we'll see.'"

"Don't you worry, darling. When that young man gets here, I'll let him know there is no way I'm sending you off late at night to drive five hours. He'll just have to wait for Sunday afternoon after church."

"I don't know if he'll want to go to church with us, Mother."

Helen looked thoughtful. "I see." She put her flowers down and sat down next to her daughter.

"Carrie, are you feeling like perhaps you're having second thoughts about marrying Andrew?"

With the question actually out in the open, Carrie chewed on her lower lip and felt the tears sting her eyes. Helen held out her arms and Carrie laid her head on her mother's shoulder and sobbed.

"He...he doesn't say 'I love you' unless, unless I ask him. And we don't have a house, and I don't want to get rid of all my things, and—" In bits and pieces, between sobs, her heart opened and all her fears spilled out.

Helen held her and listened. When the tears subsided, she reached in a pocket on her blouse and handed her daughter a tissue.

"Darling, do you love Andrew with all your heart and soul and want nothing more than to spend the rest of your life with him, wherever that leads?"

"Of course I do." Carrie felt forlorn. She shook her head slowly. "Oh Mother, I'm not sure. Maybe I just need to see him, to touch him and have his arms around me. I would be all right then."

"Would you? If you're not sure, you can always postpone the wedding. Perhaps you and Andrew still need to get to know one another. This has been pretty much of a whirlwind courtship. Marriage is a serious step. I want you to be happy with whomever you choose and if you feel you aren't sure, it would be better to wait."

"But the invitations," Carrie wailed, "all the plans that have been made, the dress, the parties. I just couldn't face Andrew's father if I did that."

"It seems to me that he sounds like the kind of man who would want you to face him with this. Surely he would understand."

"You don't know him, Mother. He is a very powerful man. Oh, I don't want you to get the wrong idea; he has been wonderful to me. I just couldn't back out now. It seemed so important to both of them that we marry in July."

"Was there any particular reason for that decision?"

"Oh, it has something to do with Andrew's thirtieth birthday."

"I see," murmured Helen again. She frowned. "This is a decision that has to be made between you and Andrew. When he gets here I suggest you find a quiet place and have a talk with him. If he loves you, he will be willing to give you time to work through this."

"You're right. I know I can talk to Andrew. Maybe it's just the wedding jitters."

Carrie sniffed and wiped her eyes again.

Helen smoothed back the hair from Carrie's face and held her chin in her hand. "I want you to know, darling, that whatever you decide, your family will be behind you, all right?"

They hugged again and Carrie got up to leave. She felt a lot better. She just needed to face her fears. She would see Andrew in three days and this was probably normal. Turning in the doorway, she gave her mother a wan smile.

"Thanks for letting me get it off my chest."

"Carrie dear, let me just say this one last thing. Turn it all over to the One who loves you unconditionally. He'll help you know what to do."

She nodded and left. As she approached the stairs again, Carrie considered her mother's request and paused. She went up to her room, closed the door, and knelt by the side of her bed.

"God, you and I have not spent much time in one another's company over the past few years. Guess I got a little busy. You know how confused I feel inside. If there is a way to work this all out, would You help me? Show me what to do, to do the right thing."

She waited, feeling a little foolish and apprehensive. To her surprise, she felt more peaceful than she had felt in a long time. A little awed, but encouraged, she went down to the kitchen and poured herself a glass of lemonade. Then, she ambled out to the porch to curl up in a shaded lounge chair and mull some questions over in her mind.

CHAPTER SIXTEEN

WEDNESDAY MORNING WAS as hot as the day before. While Carrie was trying to decide how to spend her day, her mother called from the pantry.

"Carrie, would you do a favor for me?"

"Sure, what is it?"

"Can you take this jar of spicy tomato preserves up to Nola Spencer? I promised her a jar, along with a copy of the recipe. I'd take it up myself, but at my age, a walk up that hill in this heat would do me in for sure."

Carrie took the jar and recipe with mixed emotions. It gave her something to do, but it meant going to the Spencer's and seeing Scott. He was still working on their house. Maybe she could just leave the jar and hurry home again before he knew she was there. Remembering that brotherly kiss still brought the heat to her face.

As she started out, Nubbins, who had been lying under an oak tree, got up and trotted over. He always loved a walk. He began to wag his tail and the two of them started up the hill.

Breathing the hot air, Carrie felt wilted by the time she had gone halfway. Nubbins panted heavily and his tongue hung out of his mouth. She thought of trying to send him back home, but she knew he wouldn't go. Loyal to the core, he would follow.

"Come on, old boy, you can make it. If I can walk in this heat, you can too. Come on. Good dog."

Encouraged by the cheerful tone of her voice, he wagged his tail and they continued to plod along until she reached the Spencer's house at the top of the hill. As they approached, there were the sounds of a hammer and a power saw. A couple of well-worn pickups were also in the driveway.

A dog began to bark loudly. Too late she remembered the Spencers had a dog. There went her idea of sneaking in quietly and leaving again without anyone noticing.

A brown and white spaniel ran toward them and the two dogs sniffed each other. Recognition caused more joyous barking.

The hammering stopped and the power saw was quiet. Nola Spencer appeared in the doorway of their motor home.

"Carrie! What a brave girl to come out in this heat. Come on in. I'll fix you a cold drink. Soda or lemonade?"

"Lemonade, thanks." She glanced warily toward the new addition of the house, and to her chagrin, she saw Scott was walking toward her. He wore a carpenter's apron and his T-shirt and shorts had sawdust all over them. She knew she wanted to see him.

Feeling suddenly shy and awkward, she waited for him to catch up with her.

"Well, this is a surprise. Did you come to see the new addition?"

"Oh, well, actually, my mother sent some of her spicy tomato preserves to your mother. She wanted the recipe. Mom didn't want to walk up in the heat."

If he was disappointed with her reason for being there he didn't show it. He walked with her to the motor home.

"It's about time to take a break anyway. I think I'll join you for some of my mother's cold lemonade. When you feel rested, I'll show you the addition."

"That would be nice."

They all sipped lemonade and made small talk. There was a generator on top of the motor home and cool air blew in from a vent in the ceiling. At least they weren't cooped up in small quarters and having to suffer the heat too. Carrie looked around and saw why Scott was staying in their guesthouse. There was really no room for a third person. Boxes were tucked under the dining area and clothes stacked or hung any place they would fit. How in the world two tall people like Allen and Nola Spencer could even live here seemed beyond her.

Scott downed his lemonade and waited patiently for Carrie to finish. She hastily swallowed the last of her lemonade and stood up as Nola took her glass.

"Thank you, dear, for bringing me the preserves. I can't wait to try it. Tell your mother thank you for me."

"I will."

"I'm going to show Carrie what we're accomplishing with all this mess."

"That's a good idea, Scott. You need to take a break. You've been working like a madman these last couple of weeks." She turned to Carrie. "Honestly, if we didn't say something, Scott would work half the night as well as all day. I don't know where he finds all the energy in this heat." She shook her head.

"Just want to get it done, Mom." Scott headed out the door with Carrie close behind.

"Watch your step," he warned as they headed up a plank that took them into the house. Scott showed her the new living room, with a beautiful view of the valley. The old living room would now be the family room. The small kitchen that Nola had used for years had been gutted and a porch incorporated to make a large country kitchen. The cupboards were in, waiting for the granite countertops. Scott described the appliances that would soon be installed and showed her a huge pantry. The walls of the three small bedrooms had been moved to make two large bedrooms. A master bedroom and bath had been added on the other side. Carrie, vaguely remembering the former house from a barbecue years before, marveled at the wonderfully livable house rising from the bones of the old one.

"The roof is covered with a new shingle that is fire-resistant," Scott was saying.

Carrie was impressed. "It must be wonderful to be able to build your own house the way you want it."

Scott screwed up his face and grinned. "Well, I can help with a lot of it, but," he gestured toward the men who were fitting plumbing pipe and another man who was installing metal boxes for electrical hook-ups, "it will be a while before I know enough to build one on my own."

The men had glanced up from their work to give Carrie the once over. One gave a low whistle and leaned over to comment to the man next to him.

Feeling like she was on display, she headed back toward the plank. Scott took her elbow to make sure she got down all right.

"Don't mind the guys. They always appreciate a beautiful girl, especially one in pink shorts."

They stood looking at one another. Scott's face was unreadable but she sensed herself being drawn into the depths of those dark eyes. She started to lean toward him and caught herself just in time. What was she thinking? She backed away.

"Guess I'd better be going. You have work to do."

"Right. Glad you came up, Carrie."

"Me too. Thanks for showing me around."

She turned and hurried down the driveway. Nubbins, who had been lying in the shade with the spaniel, leaped up and joined her.

Going downhill was definitely better, she decided. It wasn't any less hot, but it was easier walking. She glanced back and saw Scott still standing at the end of his driveway watching her. She waved and turned quickly away. She didn't look back again.

CHAPTER SEVENTEEN

THE STRAINS OF Grieg's "Peer Gynt Suite" poured forth from the stereo. A subtle reminder from her mother that they had many things to do today and everyone should be up. Carrie usually loved the early hours. This morning she didn't even want to look at the clock.

Her parents were usually up when the day was just beginning. When she was young she remembered watching the sun come up with her father and listening to the symphony of sounds from the various species of birds that inhabited the area at different times of the year.

As she looked out the window now, a covey of quail quickly serpentined from one side of the meadow to the other, their top-knots wobbling back and forth as they ran. Squirrels watched with bright eyes from the trees and chattered as they leaped from branch to branch.

To Carrie, morning meant the smell of the pines with the sun streaming through the branches. In the summer, the morning was the best part of the day, unless one had spent the better part of the night tossing and turning in the barest of gowns, trying to sleep in the oppressive heat.

She knew her mother would be expecting her up. At least the classical music was better than an alarm clock or pounding on one's door. When Carrie finally put in an appearance in the kitchen, she was moving in slow motion. In spite of the enticing sounds of the symphony, Carrie and her father sat silently, sipping their coffee. Helen watched them both impatiently and finally, with hands on her hips, burst out...

"I suppose neither of you have given a thought to where Andrew is going to sleep?"

Carrie blinked. "Oh. We haven't talked about it, have we?"

"I was going to bunk him in with Scott, but the trailer is so small. The only other place is Linda's room."

Carrie realized the direction her mother's thoughts were going and decided that she might as well be a volunteer as a recruit. "Linda can sleep with me. It's a double bed. We used to share in the past."

Her father beamed at her. "That's nice of you, Cricket. I know you'd probably like a room to yourself, but it would solve the problem."

Her mother shook her head. "Sharing the room would be an obvious solution, honey, but as hot as it's been, I don't think that two grown women trying to sleep on a double bed would work."

Carrie looked at her sleepily. What did she have in mind? There was no place else for anyone to sleep.

"Edna Ferguson has a roll-away bed and Carrie has plenty of space in her room. That way Linda and Carrie won't have to share the bed." Helen faced them with a triumphant smile.

"But how will we get it over here and up the stairs?" Carrie wasn't into major problem solutions at this moment.

"I called Edna this morning, you know she's up with the chickens. Her son Olen will bring it over after he gets the chores done."

Carrie pictured Olen as she remembered him from high school. Tall as a beanpole, at least six feet four and incredibly thin. She couldn't picture him wrestling the bed upstairs alone.

"...and I talked to Nola. When Olen gets here I'll just give her a jingle and Scott will come down and help get the bed upstairs."

Mike looked at his wife with a grin. "You know, honey, if I ever have any armies I need to manage, I'll recommend you for general."

"Oh, Mike!" Helen waved a hand at her husband and poured herself another cup of coffee.

Shortly after her father drove away to work, a pick-up rattled into the yard. Carrie stepped out of the laundry room with a basket full of clean sheets headed for the clothesline. Her mother was a firm believer in the fresh smell of linens dried in the sun. Olen Ferguson climbed out of the truck and waved a friendly hand at her as he opened the tailgate.

"Hi Carrie. Heard you were back. You sure have our best wishes on your wedding."

She came over to the truck. Olen had filled out considerably since the last time she saw him. He had a beard now and his eyes crinkled when he smiled. His blond hair, which usually resembled a haystack someone had run a rake through, was tamed and cut at his shoulders. He wasn't bad looking.

"Hi Olen, you've changed a bit since I saw you last."

He grinned and patted his mid-section. "Getting some good meals, she's a pretty good cook."

"Your mother?"

"Oh, I forgot. You've been away a lot. I got married two years ago. We have a little boy, Joseph, just nine months old."

She made a mental note to keep more in touch with old friends. "That's wonderful, Olen. Did you marry anyone I know?"

"Don't think so. I met her at a cousin's house in North Bend."

"Well congratulations. Sounds like a nice family. Wish I had time to see them."

"I sure understand. That's how it goes."

"Where are you living now, Olen?"

"Same place. Mom hasn't been too well lately, and didn't like rattling around in that big house by herself. It seems to be working pretty well. She and little Joe are a great team."

She was about to respond when Scott came striding down the driveway. It looked as if he had been working already. He had sawdust on his shorts. The T-shirt had obviously been thrown on for their benefit. It was clean.

"Hi Olen, how's it going? Little Joe walking yet?"

"Goin' pretty good, Scott. Joe's pulling himself up and getting into darn near everything. Becky thinks he'll take off across the room any day now. How's the house comin' along?"

"Getting there. Sure wish the heat would tone down some."

"Yeah. It's hard on my cows too."

Both men nodded as if a matter of state had been seriously considered.

"Well, let's get to it. We both have things to get back to." Scott started pulling the bed from the truck.

Carrie stood musing at this male verbal exchange, waiting for Scott to acknowledge her. As if an afterthought, he glanced at her as he and Olen wrestled the unwieldy bed out of the truck.

"Morning, Carrie. This for Andrew?"

"No, for Linda. It goes in my room. Andrew gets her room."

When they had the bed out of the truck, Olen turned to her. "Just show us the way and we'll get this baby up there."

Carrie smiled sweetly. "Oh, Scott can show you. He knows where my bedroom is. Nice to see you again, Olen." With an innocent smile, she turned her back on them, picked up the laundry basket and headed for the clothesline. The look on Scott's face was priceless.

He muttered something about luggage and she bit her lip to keep from laughing out loud as she pegged the sheets on the line.

She managed to remain out of sight until Scott had gone. Olen gave him a ride back up the hill before heading home himself.

The rollaway bed was a good brand. Carrie sat on it and bounced a couple of times. It seemed to have a firm mattress. Linda was going to take the rollaway, Carrie determined, no matter what.

The house was ready and after a quick lunch of tuna salad and fruit, Carrie headed upstairs to her room to take a nap. The house hadn't warmed up too much yet. Maybe she could make up for some of the sleep she'd lost the night before. She settled herself on her bed to read for a few moments and realized she hadn't gotten a book. Her eyes fell on the Bible lying on her nightstand. She sat up and reached for it. The marker was in Second Corinthians. Flipping it open, she started reading,

"...receive not the grace of God in vain...I have heard you in a time accepted, and in the day of salvation have I succored you; behold, now is the accepted time; behold, now is the day of salvation."

Now is the day of salvation. She had heard the prayer many times and prayed with everyone else at the church social, but had she really received Jesus as her Savior? Her mother said to ask God and He would show her. She bowed her head.

"Lord, what should I do? I feel so mixed up inside."

She waited quietly, not sure what she was waiting for. Then the scene with her grandmother, Selma Dickson, came back to her mind. Granny Dickson was putting her to bed because her parents were on a short trip. Carrie asked her how she could belong to Jesus. Granny Dickson told her that she could belong to Jesus that very night and she would show her how. Carrie knelt beside her bed and Granny knelt beside her. She repeated the words after her granny said them...*Dear Lord Jesus, I want to be Your little child. Please forgive me of my sins. Come into my heart and be my Lord and Savior. I will be Your little child always. Thank You for receiving me. Amen.*"

The warmth and happiness she felt at that moment many years before came over her again, and slipping down on her knees, she leaned her head against the side of the bed and wept for joy.

"Please forgive me for going my own way for so long."

Carrie wasn't sure how long she stayed on her knees and prayed, but when she stood up, she felt different. The heaviness was gone and in its place a quiet peace seemed to settle. With a certainty, she knew that she had placed her future in God's hands and He would show her what to do.

There was no more need for a nap. All at once she wanted to get out in the sunshine. The world looked so beautiful. The house was quiet and she slipped out and headed for the bench down by the river. She sat back on it, hugging her knees and smiling to herself.

"Am I intruding on anything?"

She turned her head and gave him a beaming smile. "No, Scott, not at all. Isn't it a beautiful afternoon?"

Puzzled, he came closer. "I saw you running down here and thought something was wrong. I was getting a clean shirt." He cocked his head to one side and studied her. "Something is different. Your face looks like sunshine. You must have talked to Andrew."

She got up and faced him. "Scott, I've talked to someone more wonderful than Andrew. I found out when I accepted Jesus. I was five years old. My Granny Dickson, my father's mother, the one who died ten years ago, helped me pray. God showed me. Isn't that wonderful?"

Scott bit his lip and looked quickly at the trees, but not before she saw the moisture in his eyes.

"Scott?"

He looked back at her and smiled. There was a look of infinite joy on his face.

"Sorry. You got me right between the eyes. I've been praying and that's a pretty speedy answer to prayer."

"You've been praying for me?" She was touched.

"Ever since the day you arrived home. You were so uptight, and unapproachable. Every time I looked at you, you turned away. You should have been on top of the world with that ring and a wedding coming up, and yet you seemed so troubled."

She put a hand on his arm. "Thank you, Scott. I think my parents have been praying too. I've had so many questions. I've been running from God, wanting to do what I wanted instead of what He wanted. Maybe I needed to come home, to familiar things, to get right with God again."

"Whatever it took, I'm really glad for you, Carrie."

She pulled him toward the bench. "Can you sit down for a little while? I just needed to share that."

"I think they can get that house built without me for a little while." He seated himself comfortably and leaned back. She felt like an eager child and Scott looked prepared to sit there all day if she wanted him to.

The river swished by and a faint breeze came up as she shared with Scott feelings she'd experienced the night of the play.

"I think God has been trying to tell me for a long time. Oh, Scott, I'm so glad I found Jesus again."

He stood up reluctantly. "I'd better get back. Thanks for sharing with me about what you found, Carrie. I feel like a pretty special friend."

"Thanks for listening to me rattle on, Scott. I guess I didn't realize you were a friend like that."

"Not only a friend but a brother," he grinned.

"A brother?"

"Sure, a brother in the Lord. We're family now."

On an impulse she reached out her arms. "Well, it's all right to hug family isn't it?"

He gave her a warm hug. Was it her imagination or was he holding her extra tight? She felt herself melt against him. It felt so good to be in his arms.

Suddenly, he pushed her away from him. "Sorry. I guess brother is one thing, human is another."

She frowned as she looked up at him, puzzled. He took a step back.

"If I don't get out of here, I'm going to find myself giving you a very un-brotherly kiss. I'd better get back to work."

He hurried up the stepping stones out of her sight, leaving her wrestling with some very un-sisterly thoughts.

CHAPTER EIGHTEEN

SHORTLY AFTER SCOTT left, a loud scrunch of gravel announced Linda's arrival. She'd gotten a day off and was able to come up Thursday afternoon to prepare things for the shower. Carrie walked up from the riverbank. Linda was driving her own small green sedan. She gave them all her courtesy hugs and grabbed a couple of leather bags out of the back seat, handing one automatically to Carrie.

"Are we ready for the big weekend?" She asked in her throaty voice, tilting her head at Carrie.

Helen laughed. "Well, I imagine we'll get it all done, but we'd better get busy, half the county is coming to the shower!"

Linda pretended to be astonished. "You mean *everyone* responded?"

"Everyone," Helen answered emphatically, "you go get settled and changed. You're in Carrie's room."

"Carrie's room?" She turned to her cousin. "And where are you sleeping?"

Carrie gave her a mischievous grin. "In my own bed. You get the rollaway."

Linda groaned. "A rollaway?"

"I'm sure you'll be comfortable, cousin. It's a pretty good mattress."

"Well in that case, why don't we trade beds?" They were heading up the stairs.

"No dice. I'm the bride. I'm sleeping in my own bed, and if you try to usurp me, you'll get dumped on the floor." Carrie deposited Linda's travel bag on the rollaway, smiled sweetly, and headed out the door, leaving her cousin staring after her, wide-eyed.

"See you downstairs."

Carrie went into the kitchen and washed her hands to set the table. Helen eyed her curiously. "You're especially chipper. Anything you care to share? Like how you have sawdust on the front of your clothes?"

Looking down, Carrie blushed. She hadn't thought to brush herself off. Her father stopped, turned around, and stood looking at Carrie expectantly. She certainly had their attention.

"I met Scott down by the river, that is, he came down after I was there. I was excited. Mother, in my room this afternoon I asked the Lord to show me when I accepted Him and He took me back one evening to a time when Granny Dickson was putting me to bed. I wanted to be Jesus' little child and she prayed with me. I accepted Jesus that night, by the side of my bed."

Her mother hugged her, pulling her handkerchief from her pocket. Her father ruffled her hair.

"You and Dad have been praying for me, haven't you?"

Helen nodded.

"Scott said he had been praying for me too. Wasn't that nice? We sat by the river and talked."

Her mother glanced at her husband. "I'm so glad you shared your discovery with him. I knew you had prayed that prayer because your grandmother told me when we got home that night. After I made a recommitment of my life to the Lord, I knew that you had to seek Him for yourself. You didn't want me telling you."

"Anyway, that's how I got the sawdust, I guess. Scott seemed so happy with my finding the Lord and all he gave me a brotherly hug. He said we're family now."

"Who's family?" Linda stood in the doorway and looked at them curiously.

"The Family of God, dear," Helen beamed. "Carrie has recommitted her life to Christ."

Linda rolled her eyes. "So you've gone religious on me too? Scott, mom and dad, and now you. Look, I'm not joining in any Bible studies or family prayer sessions, okay?"

Helen came over and put her arm around her niece's shoulders. "I've never pressured you, Linda. Any steps you take are between you and God."

She hugged her back. "I know, Mom. I guess I just feel a little ganged up on."

Being a wise woman, Helen changed the subject. "Let's have dinner, everyone, and then we can set the girls to decorating the table and folding napkins. The theme was your idea, Linda, so direct that area, okay?"

Helen reached for a stack of plates in the cupboard and handed them to Linda as Carrie got the silverware and napkins. Routine seemed to dispel Linda's defensive mood, and they all moved about the kitchen gathering the things needed. This time Carrie gave the thanks.

"How are things going at work, Linda? Is that guy still giving you problems?" Carrie had determined she was going to be friendly and see Linda in a different light.

Her cousin lit up. "As a matter of fact, he's gone, out the door on his ear, if you know what I mean."

Mike paused in the middle of buttering an ear of corn, "He got fired?"

"That's right. The boss caught him pinching clothes for his girlfriend. He thought no one knew what he was up to, but Joey, one of the stock clerks, saw him and reported it. The boss and Joey stayed late one night and caught him red-handed heading out the door with five dresses when he thought everyone had gone." Linda thumped the table with her fist. "He was canned on the spot!"

Helen patted her shoulder. "You see, Scott was right. He said you would win out in the end."

"That's true, he did. Say, where is Scott? I thought he was eating meals with you."

Helen put her fork down, "He's been working on the new addition and eating with his folks a lot."

"Hmmm. I'll have to check on his progress up there since I've been gone." She turned to Carrie who, for some reason, found herself irritated at Linda's preoccupation with Scott. "When is Andrew arriving?"

"I pick him up at the airport at three tomorrow."

"No car? I thought he was driving."

"He said he had car trouble so he's flying. Anyway, we can drive back to the city in my car."

Linda nudged her arm. "That should be a lot cozier, I would think."

Helen passed the sandwiches. "Looks like you got your car running again. It was nice of your boss to loan you his Lexus last time."

"*Her* Lexus," Linda corrected. She looked around the table at them. "Aha! Now I know what you were thinking. Girl employee gets loan of expensive car from handsome boss, with strings attached." She pointed her fork accusingly.

All three Dicksons had the grace to look guilty.

As they began to clear the table, Linda glanced at Carrie.

"Going religious seems to have given you a different outlook. How come you never challenged me before?"

"You always seemed to get your way. After a while I just stopped trying. Always thought of myself as a mouse-type, I guess."

"A mouse that roars," Linda murmured.

"The mouse that what?"

"Oh, kind of like the name of an old movie I saw on television late one night. Some little country that made war on the USA. It was rather funny."

Carrie closed up the dishwasher. "Maybe I just grew up. It just took me a little longer to find out who I was."

Linda nodded amiably and then put down the pan she was drying. "What's Andrew going to say about this new turn of yours?"

"Recommitting myself to Christ?"

"Whatever. Anyway, how do you think he'll react?"

Andrew. What would he say? Would it matter to him what she did about religion? Carrie felt uneasy for the first time since that morning. "I don't know. I'll tell him when we're alone. I'm sure he'll want me to believe the way I want to believe."

"You need to say that with more conviction, cousin." Linda leaned one hand on the edge of the sink and put the other hand on her hip. Her gaze was penetrating.

Carrie couldn't respond.

When they entered the dining room, Helen was putting a box of silk flowers on the table.

"Check out the linen cupboard, Linda, and pick out the tablecloths you want to use tomorrow. Here are some flowers and things you can look through."

She was getting ready to bake the cake, which she would decorate the next day and put into the freezer for Saturday. With Andrew coming, they wanted to have everything for the shower done so they could concentrate on having a special dinner for him tomorrow night. Helen was planning on prime rib, since Carrie mentioned he especially liked that. Stuffed baked potatoes, fresh green beans, Caesar salad, home-made rolls and fresh blackberry pie rounded out the menu. If the way to a man's heart was through his stomach, Andrew should love her family.

"Did you say Scott was coming to dinner tomorrow night, Mother?"

Helen beamed. "Yes. Don't you think that's a good idea? I thought Scott would enjoy meeting Andrew. He said he'd love to come."

Linda looked pleased and Carrie busied herself looking through the box. She wondered what the two men would think of each other.

Helen set to work in the kitchen, baking the potatoes and mixing the dough for the rolls. The fragrant blackberries which she had picked and frozen at the end of last season were now defrosting in a bowl on the table.

Linda pulled out a wine-colored tablecloth and draped it over the table. Then she placed a smaller pink one at a diagonal. She poked in the linen cupboard until she found a lace tablecloth and placed that at an opposite angle to the pink one. The three layers looked striking. Silk roses of different colors and white silk daisies were piled in a chair and these were sorted through as Linda began to arrange them on the table.

"That is definitely your forte."

Linda waved a hand casually at the table. "You think it looks all right? I like decorating. Used to do the windows of the first store I worked in."

"Really? Well, you have the flair. Me? I'm going to stick to arranging the silver and napkins, if you'll show me where you want them to go."

It was one of the few times Carrie could remember the two of them working so companionably on something. They looked at a diagram Linda had drawn of the table showing where everything was to go. Carrie was impressed. "Looks good to me."

The finished table would be a work of art. When Linda had worked everything out, she put the flowers on top of the others in the box and then carefully folded the three tablecloths that would be used on Saturday while Carrie finished folding the paper napkins.

The silver tea set was polished and sitting on the sideboard. They'd get the punch bowl and the table extensions out tomorrow.

Carrie took out the table pads and laid them on the table, covering them with a large white damask cloth. They set the table with her mother's silver and some of the serving pieces from her wedding china. With Helen's arrangement of gold silk flowers created for the centerpiece, it was an elegant table. Andrew should be impressed.

The smell of blackberry pie baking drew the cousins to the kitchen and they sat down at the oak table fanning themselves. Helen saved a small dish of blackberries that weren't needed in the pie and scooped these over vanilla ice cream. Linda and Carrie ate like starving children.

When they finished everything they could get done that evening, they wished each other good night and headed to their rooms. Linda strolled down to the guest room and opened the door to inspect the changes made for Andrew. Tan sheets with fine brown stripes were on the bed and all traces of feminine whatnots had been removed. A small low table had been placed at the end of the bed for Andrew's suitcase. The yellow towels in the bathroom had been replaced by cream-colored ones.

"Not bad…" Linda turned and went to Carrie's room. The rollaway had been made up in the soft green sheets and a gold blanket from Linda's room. She sat on the bed and grudgingly approved, but Linda had a glint in her eye and when Carrie turned her back she was hit with a pillow in the back of the head.

She whirled around. "Oh, so that's how it is!" She grabbed a pillow and flung it at Linda. Giggling like two schoolgirls, they whacked each other with the pillows. Tiny feathers began to float about the room.

The pillow fight was on in earnest when they realized the door had opened and Helen was standing there watching them with her mouth open and a look of utter astonishment on her face.

"Girls! Or should I say, ladies, it's too hot for this. Go to bed for heaven's sake." She looked at the feathers and added with a twinkle in her eyes, "and you can vacuum in the morning! Good night."

When she was gone, they collapsed in laughter.

"I haven't had so much fun in ages," Linda gasped.

"Me too."

"Who gets the first shower?"

"Go ahead, Linda, I'll straighten up this mess."

When Carrie finished her own shower she came back to the room expecting to have to roust Linda out of her bed, but her cousin was sitting on the rollaway, glancing through a magazine.

Finally, they sprawled on top of the covers of their beds in the darkness.

"Carrie?"

"Hmm?"

"Have you and Andrew ever, you know—"

This time Carrie didn't feel the need to sound sophisticated. "No," she answered softly.

"Not ever?"

"No. He wanted to, but I had this thing that I wanted to wait until our wedding night. He wasn't too happy but he respected my wishes."

"Well in this day and age, that's admirable."

"Linda, have you ever…?"

There was a long silence and Carrie thought she wasn't going answer. Finally there was a heavy sigh. "I wish I hadn't."

"I'm sorry, Linda. I didn't mean to pry. It's just that I'm a little nervous, I guess."

"If he really loves you, you'll be all right. It will be great."

"Was it great?"

"I loved him terribly. Too bad I found out that the rat was married, with four kids! I talk a lot and I know I flirt, but as far as I'm concerned it will be a long time before I trust anyone like that again."

"You don't want to be hurt."

"Who does? Maybe one day my Mr. Right will come along and I'll change my mind, but there are a lot of takers out there. They take you to dinner and think you owe them."

"I had that happen once. It was a greasy hamburger and a lousy movie, and he wanted to come in. I just thanked him for the evening and quickly shut the door. He was pretty miffed."

"Good for you, cousin. That's the only way to treat those guys."

"You've never met anyone else you were interested in?"

Linda sighed. "Oh, there was a guy once. There was something about him. I put him in a cab outside a party. He'd had a few too many, but he was cute, and nice. He called me his 'golden angel.' I never found out who he was, but I remembered him for a long time."

"Maybe you'll meet him again."

"Yeah." There was silence again, but Carrie knew Linda wasn't sleeping.

"Linda, do you really like Scott, or do you just like to flirt with him?"

"He's a little too much on the religious side for me, but he's nice." She yawned sleepily. "I never could resist flirting with a good-looking man. He's more your type, cousin. Boy, I'm beat. Goodnight."

Linda's remark about Scott had been off-hand and they'd laughed, but now Carrie lay there in the darkness. *Scott is more your type.* She felt his arms around her again and thought of his last words, "I might find myself giving you an un-brotherly kiss."

The realization slowly crept into her consciousness like wine warming her body. How could she have not seen or realized what was happening? How she felt when she was near him. How she wanted him to hold her. She bit her lip to keep from crying out. She was committed to Andrew. There was no backing out now. How could she just call everything off and upset so many people? Scott must never know how she felt. After all, didn't he have a girl, somewhere? It wasn't Margo, but he had intimated as much, someone down in the valley near his school. Scott was kind. She couldn't bear to see pity in his eyes.

Resolving to be strong for all the wrong reasons, she let the tears slide down her cheeks in the darkness. Soft snores told her Linda had fallen asleep. Carrie buried her head in her pillow and wept silently for what could never be.

CHAPTER NINETEEN

LINDA WAS STILL asleep, one arm flung across her pillow. Carrie tiptoed quietly around, getting dressed. Andrew was coming today. Her chest felt constricted. Two weeks ago she would have hardly been able to bear the hours until she saw him. Now, she felt like a vast whirlpool was drawing her in and she was helpless to prevent it.

She went in the bathroom and whispered, "Lord, please help me through this day. I don't know what to do. I don't know what to say. I feel so confused again. Please be with me and give me Your strength and wisdom. I put this whole marriage in Your hands… Your will be done, Lord."

Feeling a little better, she slipped out and went downstairs to the kitchen. To her surprise her mother was up, absorbed in decorating the cake. She finished a rose and glanced up.

"Oh. Sorry, darling, deep at work here. Didn't see you come in." She looked at her daughter more closely. "Did you sleep well?"

"Yes, finally. I seem to have a hard time waking up here."

"You probably just needed the rest, dear. Too much activity in the city."

"Probably."

"How about some breakfast? I can scramble you some eggs and—"

"Mother, you are a dear. It's nice having you cook for me, but I'm a big girl. I can get my own breakfast." Carrie tempered her words with a grin and a kiss on her mother's cheek.

"Oh, of course I know that. It's just that I don't get much of a chance to do for you and who knows when I'll have an opportunity in the future. You and Andrew will be so busy with your social life in San Diego."

Don't falter now, Carrie, get a grip on yourself. "Yes, I guess you're right." She gave her mother a bright smile. "How about poached eggs on toast?"

Helen got out the egg poacher and put a slice of whole wheat bread in the toaster as Carrie poured herself some orange juice. This morning she eyed the coffeepot. A cup of strong black coffee wouldn't hurt.

Her mother went to the pantry and came back with her arms loaded. She dumped the items on the sink, and took the prime rib roast out of the refrigerator. She'd gotten it out of the freezer the afternoon before to defrost. There was enough room in the pantry to put the big freezer, but getting it in there had been a major task. The lid and hinges had to be removed as well as the door frame. The freezer was pulled through with barely a quarter of an inch to spare on either side. It was well worth the effort though to have it so handy.

Helen looked around the kitchen. "Where's Linda?"

"Still sleeping, I guess."

"Well, go roust her, we've got things to do."

Carrie went dutifully upstairs to her bedroom. When she peeked around the bedroom door she saw Linda was already awake.

"What did someone put in the coffee last night? I slept like a rock."

"I think we both did. Mother says it's our busy city life and we are catching up on our rest. You know, just one mad, exciting party after another."

Linda grinned wryly. "Laugh now, cousin. It won't be long before that's just what you'll be doing. It doesn't sound like the Van Zants like to spend a lot of time watching television. As the main female, guess who's going to be hostess for all that?"

Carrie sat down on her bed suddenly and stared at the carpet. "I don't know if I'm up to that life, Linda."

"Whoa, you aren't by any chance getting cold feet, are you?"

"Oh, no, just getting a little overwhelmed with it all. I'll be okay."

"Now Carrie, lover boy is arriving today and after a few hugs and kisses you will hardly be able to wait for that wedding."

After a few hugs and kisses Andrew will know something is wrong.

"You're right. I can hardly wait to see him." She mustered as much enthusiasm in her voice as she could.

Linda gave her a searching look, but didn't comment. She got up and opened her suitcase, pulling out some slacks and a casual shirt.

Carrie hurried downstairs knowing her breakfast was probably ready, which it was.

"Linda's up and dressing. She'll be down in a few minutes."

"Thank you, dear."

She poured herself a cup of coffee and changed her mind on having it black when she spied the French vanilla creamer on the table.

After Linda had eaten, they vacuumed, dusted, made beds, fetched and carried, and ran errands as Helen directed. Linda was surprisingly agreeable to whatever needed to be done. Carrie glanced at her from time to time. It was as if, now that they were grown, she could see her cousin differently. Linda had only bullied her because she could. Something was healed between them and Carrie no longer resented her.

Mike Dickson had been astonished to hear of the goings on the night before. "A pillow fight? Linda and Carrie?"

"If I hadn't opened that door to find out what the commotion was all about and seen it with my own eyes, I never would have believed it either. Two grown women and they both looked like they were about ten years old!" Helen glanced at Linda, who, with her make-up on and dressed, looked every inch the mature, sophisticated woman.

The two cousins looked at each other with exaggerated innocence. Linda winked and Carrie winked back.

The day fairly flew and at one-thirty Carrie was racing to her room to change. It was an hour to the airport. Andrew didn't like pants on women, so she tossed a simple, cool sheath dress on the bed and jumped into the shower. In twenty minutes she was racing down the stairs with her car keys.

"I know you are anxious, darling, but do drive carefully. You have time."

"I know. I just don't want to be late."

She had sprayed on a touch of Obsession. Andrew had given it to her, and while she didn't care for the name too much, if he liked the scent, she would use it. An hour was a long time to think. How would she feel when she saw him? Would all these jitters be for nothing? Was she wrong about her feelings for Scott? Maybe she was just feeling a little lonesome.

The car fairly flew down the mountain. She paid no attention to the scenery for the fears and questions that assailed her mind. When she raced into the terminal, to her immense relief the plane hadn't landed yet. Too nervous to sit, she wandered around the small lobby looking at pictures of airplanes on the walls. The loudspeaker announced that the plane had just touched down and would be arriving at the gate shortly.

In about five minutes she saw the light plane taxi down the runway close to the airport and swing around into position. Andrew was the last person to get off the plane.

A pilot was assisting him down the steps. He let go of Andrew's elbow when they reached the ground, and as they got closer, she could see that they were chatting amiably. The pilot gave him a pat on the shoulder and headed toward another part of the terminal.

"Hi, baby." Andrew strolled toward her and slipped an arm around her waist, kissing her in front of an amused group of passengers. His breath smelled of liquor.

"Oh, Andrew, are you all right? I saw the pilot helping you off the plane. Were you sick?"

"Don't like small planes. Guess I'm a white-knuckler anytime I have to fly in one. Had a couple of gin and tonics to get me through. They just wanted to be sure I got off all right. Nice people."

Carrie suspected he'd had more than just a couple. A knot formed in the pit of her stomach. She never saw them serve a passenger more than one on the one hour flight. She kept silent, determined to be as loving as she could be. Perhaps if she took her time, he'd feel better by the time they got home.

"Whew. Is it any cooler up in the mountains? This heat wave is getting to me."

"It's getting to all of us, Andrew. It has to break soon. The guest room is the coolest room in the house."

"Guest room? He leered at her. "Gonna share it with me?"

"Andrew!"

"Oh yes. Forgot. No hanky-panky till the wedding night." He wagged a finger at her as she took his arm and steered him toward the baggage claim. The suitcase seemed overly large for just one weekend.

"My goodness, what did you bring?"

"Don't know. Davis packed it. Just told him a weekend in the mountains."

"Davis?"

"Our butler."

"Oh." Was she going to have a personal maid when they got married? She wasn't sure she wanted someone laying out all her clothes and deciding what she should wear.

"Also brought a gift for your folks."

"Oh, Andrew, how thoughtful of you."

They loaded the car and Andrew got in the passenger side, stretching out his long legs and putting his arm on the back of the seat.

"Drive me to the country, woman."

She was relieved. At least he didn't have a hang-up on women drivers. She wasn't about to let him drive.

Pointing out landmarks, she took the long way through town. Andrew wouldn't know the difference, and it was the only way she knew to buy time.

As they started up the winding mountain road she could hardly wait until they got to the lake. She hoped Andrew would be impressed. As they rounded a curve, the lake sparkled in front of them and Andrew whistled.

"That's a sight. Ever go sailing on it?"

Pleased with his response, she shook her head. "Never knew anyone who had a sailboat."

"We'll just have to buy one and go sailing. Too bad there's not enough time this weekend."

She shook her head at him. "Andrew, you are impossible. I think you really would go buy a sailboat."

"What's money for, except to spend?"

Carrie felt a touch of irritation. There were a lot of good things he could do with all that money besides spending it on himself. She shrugged.

"Let's see, your mother owns a bookshop of some sorts, her name is Helen, right?" She nodded. "And your father works for the Forestry Service, puts out fires and stuff—name's Mike." She nodded. "There's a whole lot more than putting out fires, Andrew, it's about managing our resources."

He pursed his lips. "Then, there's you, and who else?"

"My cousin Linda. Remember, I told you about her."

"She lives there too?"

"No, in the Bay Area. She just came to put the shower together for the weekend, and of course meet you."

"Sounds good to me."

"Oh, my mother invited a neighbor, Scott Spencer, to join us for dinner."

Andrew frowned. "Do I have to talk about crops and chickens?"

"Andrew! He's not a country bumpkin. He teaches high school down in Napa Valley and coaches the football team. He's living in our trailer, we call it the guest house, while his folks finish remodeling their house."

"How old is this school teacher?"

"Well, he was two years ahead of me in school."

"So he's been hanging around the whole time you've been home?" He was looking straight ahead.

She sighed. "Actually he spends most of his time working on the remodeling job. He took Linda up to see the project. I didn't go with them." Well, that part at least was true.

She wanted to change the way the conversation was going, but Andrew came out of his mood as quickly as he had fallen into it and gave her his beguiling grin.

He lay his head back on the seat. "Smells pretty good up here. I could get used to this country air." He moved one finger lazily along her neck and around her ear.

"Andrew! I'm trying to drive the car."

"Mmmm? Just seeing if you can be distracted."

"Of course I can. I just don't want to run off the road into one of those ravines."

He glanced over at the steep incline. "Look, no hands," he grinned as he moved over to his side of the car. "Oh, I brought you some wedding invitations. Dad said you might have a few people to invite."

"A few? How many did you bring?"

He made a face. "I don't know. Maybe a dozen or so."

"Why didn't you call me and ask me how many we needed?"

"Only a few people in your family. Didn't think you'd need a lot. Besides, baby, you can't invite the whole town, not enough room."

"But there is room for all the people your father has invited?" She couldn't keep the irritation out of her voice.

"Whoa. My kitten has sprouted some claws. What's the big deal?"

She pulled over to the side of the road and stopped the car. "Andrew Van Zant, your father has planned the whole wedding, even to picking out my wedding dress and the dress my cousin Linda will wear. He's hired the caterer, reserved the church, and no one has even asked me how many friends I want to invite to my own wedding!" She felt the tears rising to the surface.

He pulled her into his arms and held her. "Whoa, babe, I'm sorry. We thought you wouldn't mind having things planned. I just wanted things to be great for you."

She sniffed and blew her nose on the hanky he'd offered. "You and your father mean well, Andrew, but a girl usually plans on getting married only once. It's the most important day of her life. I wanted some part in the wedding and I've had no say at all, on anything. I thought it didn't matter, but it does."

He kissed her eyes and her nose and then kissed her thoroughly on the mouth. She gave up arguing with him and let herself be kissed, but she felt no passion at all. Andrew drew back and studied her face a moment, but said nothing. She had tried to respond to him as she always had before but it wasn't the same. She didn't want to consider any other options at the moment.

"You okay, baby?"

She put the car in gear and moved out on the highway again. "I'm fine, Andrew, I'm just a little nervous."

"We'll get this shower business over with and head back to the city. You'll feel better when we have some people around. We're invited to the Montigo's next Friday for a dinner party. Never could stand him, but they usually have some interesting guests. They put on a good party."

Another party with more boring people wandering around with a drink in their hand. Men who got a little too familiar after a couple of martinis and women who talk about how difficult it is to get a good maid these days. How could she have thought it was so exciting?

"That's nice, Andrew."

"That's my girl. How much farther to Lewiston?"

"Just a few miles, you'll see the sign."

They turned off the highway and drove down into the small valley that held the little town of Lewiston in its palm. She pointed out the post office and when they passed a couple of deer by the side of the road, Andrew made a rifle out of his two arms and pretended to draw a bead on them.

"Hey, looks like you've got hunting grounds right on your doorstep."

"Not unless you want to get closely acquainted with the game warden."

"No hunting?"

"The whole valley is posted. The deer are tame. Besides, what kind of a sport is it to walk up to a tame deer and shoot it?"

He gave an exaggerated sigh and lowered his "rifle."

Carrie slowed down for a covey of quail that had started across the road. With a flurry of wings, they flew into nearby bushes. Andrew raised his eyebrows and nodded toward the bushes. She laughed and shook her head.

"No quail either. What do you folks find to do up here, watch the grass grow?"

She arched one eyebrow. "A lot more things than you city folks think."

They turned down the gravel road and began to cross the bridge. Andrew looked at both sides of the narrow span. "Is this the only access to your place?"

"Yep."

"Sure would hate to tackle this on a dark night. How deep is that river?"

"Oh Andrew, the bridge is wide enough. Anyway, those cables would hold any car that strayed near the edge."

"You've got to be kidding."

"No, really. A big dump truck came across and a tire went over the edge. The cable held that truck."

He chewed his lip and eyed her skeptically. "Let's just get across, okay?"

They pulled up in front of the house and Nubbins barked furiously.

"Nubbins! He's a friend, now stop that!"

Nubbins quieted down at the sound of her voice and sniffed Andrew's pant leg as he gingerly stepped from the car. It was obvious that he wasn't used to dogs.

Her parents came out on the porch. Helen was beaming expectantly but her father had on his "we'll wait and see" face.

Andrew got his suitcase out of the back seat and set it down on the ground as he turned around.

"Mother, Dad, this is my fiancé, Andrew Van Zant. Andrew, my parents, Helen and Mike Dickson."

Helen gave him a warm hug, "Andrew, we are so glad to meet you. Welcome to our mountain community."

Andrew, more used to Linda's brand of social hugs was a little surprised, but hugged her back.

Mike extended his hand and Andrew shook it solemnly, glancing down at the strength of the grip. "Delighted to meet you, sir."

"We're glad to meet you, son

Carrie looked around for Linda and figured she was probably waiting inside. Linda liked grand appearances.

Helen gestured toward the house. "Why don't you get Andrew settled in his room? Dinner will be ready in a little while."

Andrew picked up his suitcase and with an arm around Carrie, followed the Dicksons into the house.

Linda was waiting at the foot of the stairs looking absolutely smashing in mauve slacks and a cream blouse. She was wearing her gold earrings and bracelets. She started to put a hand out, and then, her eyes widened. She stepped back. "It's you! *You're* Andrew Van Zant?"

Carrie felt a knot in the pit of her stomach. "You and Andrew know each other?"

Linda regained her composure, but her eyes never left Andrew's face. "We met, once, a long time ago. I didn't know his name."

Andrew, who had been staring at Linda like he'd found the pot of gold at the end of the rainbow, threw back his head and laughed, a deep, rich laugh. "*You* were the one. A gold dress that shimmered in the moonlight, and that golden hair. I didn't know who you were when you put me in that taxi. Tried to find out, but no one seemed to know your name. He took a step toward Linda. "I called you my golden angel."

CHAPTER TWENTY

*T*HERE WAS A shocked silence. Carrie stared at her cousin. "He's the one you told me about? The one you put in a cab that night?"

Linda nodded.

Helen moved protectively by Carrie's side as they all focused on Linda.

"What?" Linda looked at their serious faces and laughed. "For heaven's sake. It was a long time ago. Long before he met Carrie." Cocking her head to one side, she glanced slyly at Andrew. "Our friend here had a little too much to drink at a party. I was leaving at the same time he was, or at least I think he was trying to leave. He just needed some assistance."

Carrie's father frowned. "You took him home?"

"Of course not, Dad, I put him in a cab. There was a hotel key in his pocket, so I told the cab driver to take him to that hotel. They'd take care of him from there."

"Oh, so you went through my pockets." Andrew was still smiling at her and not in the least abashed that she'd told them he'd had too much to drink.

"The key was in the first pocket I looked in, buddy. I didn't look further."

Carrie and her parents listened to this exchange in stunned silence. Carrie finally stepped forward, put her arm possessively through Andrew's and smiled sweetly at her cousin.

"Well, that was a nice thing to do, Linda. I'll show my fiancé to his room now. We'll see you in a little while." She looked expectantly at Andrew.

"Hmmm? Oh. Sure, babe, let's get me settled." Andrew was still distracted by Linda. He tore his eyes away from her face reluctantly and picked up the suitcase he'd dropped suddenly. Carrie all but pulled him up the stairs.

When they reached the guest room and closed the door, she searched his face. "Andrew?"

He grinned and pulled her into his arms. "Hey, I missed you, baby. Don't get all uptight. It was just one of those things."

"Are you sure, Andrew? I saw the way you were looking at her. I don't know what in the world my parents are thinking right now."

He kissed her and let his hands slide down her back. "You're the one I'm marrying, okay? Loosen up."

She pressed against him, but when he wanted to kiss her again, she put her hands against his chest. "I don't know what to think, Andrew."

He cocked his head and studied her face. "I hope things are going to be a little warmer when we're married, babe. The last thing I want is a cold fish for a wife."

Shocked at his words, she jerked away from him, close to tears.

"There's just too much going on."

He pulled her against him again and his voice took on a soothing tone. "It's okay, babe. It's okay."

Somewhat mollified, she nodded. "Maybe it's just wedding nerves. Let's get you unpacked." What was she trying to prove? She had to think and pray, but this was not the time.

He straightened his tie and ran a hand through his hair. "Sure. That would be great."

Davis had evidently not been filled in on what kind of a country weekend Andrew was going off to. He had packed for the usual social weekend at someone's large country estate.

"Well, Andrew, if we have tennis or a grand ball or go grouse hunting, you'll have everything you need."

He scratched d his head. "Guess I should have given him a little more information."

They hung what he needed in the closet and left the rest in the suitcase. Andrew pulled a package from the bottom of the suitcase.

"A gift for dinner" he announced. "Of course, I'll be more than glad to share it." He unwrapped the package to reveal a large bottle of expensive wine. He held it up triumphantly.

Dismayed, she stared at the bottle. A gift for her parents. She should have realized what Andrew would bring. He was looking thoughtfully at the gold foil on top of the bottle.

"Imagine that girl being your cousin Linda."

Carrie watched his face. This weekend was going to be a lot different than she had anticipated.

"Well, let's go celebrate." With long strides, Andrew started toward the stairs, a bit too eager for Carrie's way of thinking. She followed quickly behind him.

"Mrs. Dickson, something for you and your husband." With a flourish, he presented her mother with the wine.

Helen smiled and took the bottle as Andrew turned toward the dining room and saw Linda. "Sure looks good" he said enthusiastically, but it wasn't clear whether he was referring to the dinner table or the woman who was lighting the candles. He didn't see the exchange of looks behind his back.

"Andrew, would you like some wine with dinner?"

"Sure, let's have a glass all around."

"We're just waiting for another guest, Scott Spencer."

"Ah yes, Carrie told me you invited a neighbor. A school teacher. That was nice of you, Mrs. Dickson, I'll look forward to meeting him." He gave them his most charming smile, but his eyes lingered on Linda.

There was a knock at the front door, and Mike went to let Scott in. He was wearing a short-sleeved tan dress shirt, a tie, and brown slacks. He looked wonderfully handsome.

Carrie took Andrew's arm and drew him forward. "Andrew, this is Scott Spencer. Scott, my fiancé, Andrew Van Zant."

The two men gripped each other's outstretched hand, silently appraising one another.

Linda and Scott sat opposite Andrew and Carrie with Carrie's parents each taking their places at the ends of the table. Helen had put a wineglass in front of Andrew and had a couple more on the sideboard.

"Anyone else joining me? I know you won't have any, babe."

Carries' parents both smiled politely and shook their heads.

Carrie was uncomfortable. *I've got to talk to Andrew later.*

He turned to Scott, bottle ready. "How about you?"

"Sorry, Andrew. Not for me. You go ahead, though."

Linda picked up a glass and held it out. "I'll join you, Andrew." She gave her aunt and uncle a quick, defiant look.

Visibly relieved, Andrew filled her glass up, and they lifted their glasses in a silent toast.

When they were all seated, Carrie reached over and took Andrew's hand, squeezing it to get his attention. He glanced at her with one eyebrow cocked.

She bowed her head and he looked around the table quickly taking in the situation. Then, his eyes rested on Linda. She gave him a half smile and a slight shrug as she bowed her head. Andrew set his wineglass down and dutifully bowed his head.

Mike's blessing was brief, but he thanked the Lord for Andrew's safe journey and arrival and blessed the hands that prepared the meal. When it was over, everyone seemed to have the same idea, to make Andrew feel at ease. Dishes were passed around and he hardly had time to sip his wine.

The salad was an inspired creation of Helen's, with garbanzo beans, avocado, tomato, three kinds of lettuce, and sliced olives.

As they ate, Andrew looked over at Scott. "So you teach high school? Carrie says you went to school together."

"We were in high school at the same time. I was a couple of years ahead of her."

"He was the star quarterback, Andrew," Carrie chipped in, somehow wanting to bolster Scott's image in Andrew's eyes.

Linda watched Carrie and Andrew thoughtfully. As she returned Andrew's gaze, Carrie watched her, knowing that particular look—bold, provocative, and possessive. She was openly flirting with Andrew! Then, remembering their conversation the night before, when Linda said she just liked to flirt, Carrie relaxed, but only a little. Linda said she had been hurt too badly to take any man seriously right now. It was small comfort, though, because Carrie could sense something going on. Something between the two of them she couldn't put her finger on, and Andrew had called Linda his "golden angel."

She turned to pick up the conversation. Scott was talking, "…so I coach the team and we did pretty well, won the playoffs."

Carrie broke in brightly. "Andrew brought some wedding invitations for us, Mother. He picked them up at the engravers."

"That's wonderful, Andrew. Thank you. I need to get busy and get them out. Did Carrie tell you how many we needed?"

Andrew looked a little sheepish. "I'm sorry. I only brought about a dozen." He gave Carrie a rueful glance. "I'll have Dad send you some more, overnight express."

"That would be very kind, Andrew. We would probably need quite a few more. I was hoping to get them before this. The wedding is only three weeks away." It was a gentle, but firm rebuke.

Mike had been unusually silent. Now he turned to Andrew and cleared his throat. "Have you found a house or apartment for the two of you yet?"

Andrew looked puzzled. "Didn't Carrie tell you? We're going to live in my family home." He shrugged. "No need to let my dad rattle around in that big house by himself."

"I see." Mike managed to incorporate a lot of thoughts in two words. "At least you don't have to worry about Carrie burning your dinners. She's a good cook."

"Oh, we have a cook. She might be a bit miffed to have someone else interfering in her kitchen."

"You also have a housekeeper?" Linda drawled.

Andrew knew an inquisition when he heard it. He put down his fork and gave them his winning smile.

"Now, none of you have to worry about Carrie. She'll be well taken care of, I can assure you."

Mike didn't smile back. He gave Andrew another piercing look. "What exactly will she do?"

Carrie broke in with a tone of desperation. "Daddy, will you please pass the rolls? They are great."

Her father got the message along with a sharp look from his wife. He closed his mouth. Helen went into the kitchen and carried in two plates of prime rib. She placed a slice of medium rare meat in front of Andrew according to Carrie's directions the day before. It looked succulent and tender with peppercorns tucked in for extra flavor.

Andrew eyed his slice appreciatively. "On second thought, if Carrie cooks like her mother, we may fire the cook!"

Everyone laughed and the tension was broken, but only temporarily. Scott had remained quiet after Helen broke in. Andrew reached for the wine bottle, but Linda demurred after a second glass, so he shrugged and filled his own again. He had downed two glasses already.

Carrie started to get up and help serve, but her mother insisted that she remain by their guest.

Andrew leaned back and spoke magnanimously about the import business and a large estate they had recently secured, giving them authority to sell the contents. The owners had a collection of opaline glass that was priceless, along with some seventeenth-century furniture. He spoke of some of the innovations he was trying to persuade his father to consider in the coming year, but his speech was getting slurred. Scott asked a few casual questions and gave Andrew his complete attention.

Carrie observed Linda and nervously glanced at Andrew. Scott watched Andrew refill his glass and glanced at Carrie. Andrew, having more wine than the dinner could offset, lowered his guard, and openly admired Linda. And, with mounting dismay, Mike and Helen watched them all.

When Helen brought out the plates of blackberry pie topped with homemade vanilla ice cream, they all groaned. Though protesting how full they were, they ate everything to the last crumb.

Andrew looked around the table, satiated. "How about an after-dinner liqueur to top off a great meal?"

Helen patted him on the arm as she was getting up to clear the table. "I'm so sorry, Andrew, but we don't have anything like that in the house."

"Well, Mrs. Dickson, after a meal like that, I can forgive you." He grinned at her and turned to Carrie. "Remind me to pick something up tomorrow, okay, babe?"

"Andrew, we don't usually have after dinner drinks at our house."

Bright-eyed, he leered at them all. "Hmmm. Did notice a few teetotalers. None of you drink anything, 'cept Linda?"

They all shook their heads.

Helen began gathering up plates. "Why don't the two of you get some nice fresh air? It's a beautiful evening." She looked pointedly at Carrie.

Carrie put her arm though Andrew's as he stood up a little unsteadily. She forced herself to sound cheerful. "That's a wonderful idea. Come see our river, Andrew."

He swayed a bit and drew a pack of cigarettes from his pocket. Mike started to rise from his chair, his face grim. At this point Scott got up quickly and came around the table.

"How about Andrew and I checking out the river? You girls have a few things to do. We'll be back in a little while."

Mike took a deep breath, nodded to Scott and slowly sat down again, his eyes on Andrew. "Thank you, son."

Carrie was more relieved than she realized. She couldn't hold Andrew up by herself. Scott would take charge of him. Maybe a walk in the evening air would help Andrew feel better. She gave Scott a grateful look.

Taking Andrew's elbow, Scott steered him to the front door.

"Hey, great idea, old man. You're not as pretty, but we can get acquainted." Andrew stopped and leaned toward Linda. "How about you, golden angel, want to join us?"

"I'll pass, Andrew. We'll get the dishes done while you two men have a walk."

She paused and spoke more softly, "Don't fall in the river, buddy."

Tears of frustration threatened to well up in Carrie's eyes, but Linda took her by the arm. "You're drying, cousin," she said firmly, and led her into the kitchen.

Helen's mouth had a grim set as she rinsed dishes and placed them in the dishwasher with a vengeance. Mike and Linda began to bring dishes in from the dining room. While he didn't speak, Carrie knew her dad was agitated.

Working together in the kitchen had usually been an occasion for light conversation, but now a pall of silence hung over the room.

Finally, her mother could stand it no longer. "Carrie, does Andrew have a drinking problem?"

Defensive, Carrie shook her head. "He had a couple of drinks on the plane because he's terrified of flying in small aircraft. I think it's just a combination of that and the wine with dinner."

Linda stopped with a platter in her hand and faced Carrie, her eyes flashing. "You can't be that naïve. He wasn't on the small plane at the dinner table, and he downed that wine like it was the last bottle on earth!"

Carrie opened her mouth to respond angrily, but a parade of scenes passed before her eyes; Andrew at dinner parties and other social gatherings they'd gone to. A drink usually in his hand and the bright eyes that told her he'd had a few more than he said he'd had. Did she only see what she wanted to see? Her lower lip trembled and her eyes stung with tears.

Helen dried her hands quickly and put an arm around her daughter's shoulders. "Darling, we are only concerned for you because we love you. Andrew is charming and he's everything you said he was. It's just that the problem must be faced. It won't go away just because you don't want to see it."

Carrie looked at them and flung her dishtowel over a chair. "I don't want to talk about this any more. I'm going to look for Andrew."

She ran out of the kitchen and jerked open the front door only to find herself face to face with Scott and Andrew. Andrew could barely stand up. Scott's face held barely concealed anger.

"Where's the guest room, Carrie? I think your fiancé needs to get some sleep. He'll be fine in the morning."

Wordlessly, she turned and headed up the stairs. Scott hung on to Andrew, who stumbled several times getting up the stairs. She opened the door to the guest room and Scott maneuvered Andrew over to the bed and lowered him down.

"I need to talk to him, Scott," she began, but Scott's dark look cut her off.

"He's in no condition to carry on a conversation with anyone, Carrie. Go downstairs. I'll put him to bed."

"I could help," she tried again, but Scott turned from Andrew and, taking her by the arm, propelled her to the door, put her outside, and closed it firmly behind her.

She paused in the hall, torn between running to her own room and giving vent to tears or going downstairs to talk to her mother. She simmered. *Who does Scott Spencer think he is? He has no right...* yet even as the thoughts jumbled in her mind, she knew Scott was right. It was not her place to put Andrew to bed here. A nagging thought assailed her. *If we marry, how many times will I be the one to put him to bed like that?* She sat down suddenly at the top of the stairs and wrapped her arms around her knees.

Presently Scott came out and quietly shut the door. He eased himself down beside her and glanced sideways, gauging his welcome.

"I'm sorry. I didn't mean to be so gruff. Guess I was a little angry with Andrew for pulling this scene tonight. I knew how important it was for you, first impression and all."

She couldn't look at him. "That was a nice thing to do, Scott." She wondered if she sounded as anguished and forlorn as she felt.

"Hey, what's a brother for anyhow?" He reached up and gently pulled her head down on his shoulder, handing her his handkerchief as her body shook with silent tears.

She mopped her eyes and lifted her head, but stayed in the comforting circle of his arm. There were so many things she wanted to say and she didn't know where to begin.

"Is this a private affair or can anyone join the wake?" Linda stood at the foot of the stairs looking up at them with her hands on her hips. She gave them a long, knowing look.

Scott removed his arm and stood up, as did Carrie. "Don't get any wrong ideas, Linda."

"Oh, I don't have any wrong ideas. I'm not blind."

"Linda, let it go," Scott almost growled at her. He started down the stairs. "It's time I was getting home anyway. He brushed past her and after stopping in the kitchen to briefly thank Helen for the dinner, he let himself out.

Carrie walked past Linda without looking at her and went toward the kitchen, where she overheard her parents arguing.

"...can't let her marry someone like that!"

"Now Mike, she's a grown woman, she has to see that for herself."

Her mother and father were sitting at the kitchen table having a cup of coffee. At the sight of his daughter, Mike was quiet, but shook his head and stared down at his coffee. At least, Carrie noted, his face didn't look like a thundercloud any more. Helen looked up at Carrie, her eyes filled with concern.

"Is Andrew all right, darling?"

"I'm sure he'll be fine in the morning, Mom."

"Would you like some coffee?" Her father had his hand on the pot.

Carrie smiled weakly. "Thanks, Daddy, maybe that would be a good idea."

He poured her a cup. "Your mother and I have solved a whale of a lot of problems over a cup of coffee. Helps you think. Right, honey?"

"We've had a few of our own to solve, that's true." She turned to her daughter. "How are you feeling?"

"A little shaky. It was nice of Scott to take care of Andrew."

"Yes, dear, he is a kind young man."

"He put Andrew to bed."

"I thought he did."

Helen broke in. "Do you want to cancel tomorrow, Carrie?"

She shook her head. "I couldn't do that."

Helen took her hand. "Carrie. I know this is a difficult situation for you. Will you promise me you will pray about it? I'm not asking for any sudden decisions. You know God can work in Andrew's life just as He has worked in yours. You made a re-commitment to Christ. Andrew must know of that commitment before you are married, for that will affect many things you do as his wife. Will you do that? Will you give it to the Lord? He'll show you what to do."

Hanging her head, she answered softly, "Yes, I'll pray. I know God can help Andrew. And I want to help him any way I can."

Helen patted her arm and gave her husband a tentative smile. It was enough for now. "Good girl. Now let's get moving. We have things to do for tomorrow."

Linda had been standing in the kitchen doorway, listening. At Helen's last words, she turned and headed for the linen cupboard.

Mike got up and after giving Carrie a brief hug, went to his den.

"Come on, cousin, I need a slave to carry out my orders."

Carrie rolled her eyes and followed after Linda. In a few moments she was spreading out tablecloths and following directions as Linda re-created the beautiful table she had arranged the night before. This time the silver tea set and the punch bowl were in place on the table. Carrie took the folded napkins and arranged them as she was shown. Linda arranged the silver forks. As Carrie worked, she began to view the evening in a better light. Everything would be better tomorrow. She'd talk to Andrew and everything would be all right.

With the decorations put up, the table set, the cake ready in the freezer, and the punch base mixed, there was nothing more to do. They wearily headed for bed.

Carrie paused at the top of the stairs, thinking to see if Andrew was all right, but as she started that direction, Linda took her arm.

"Let him sleep. In the morning he'll shave and shower and be ready to face all of us again." She let out a long sigh. "Let him sleep." Linda's face held almost a wistful look.

Carrie let herself be drawn to her room. When they were at last in their beds with the light out, the darkness seemed to lay heavily on them with the still oppressive heat.

"That was a pretty tender scene on the stairs."

"You mean with Scott?"

"Now, who else were you sitting cozily with? You know he's in love with you."

Carrie gasped. "Oh Linda, you're wrong. He was just being kind."

"Don't be naïve. I know what I saw when he looked at you. Did you ever consider that you might be marrying the wrong man?"

"Linda! I'm marrying Andrew because I love him. He loves me. You mustn't talk like this."

"I just want you to think about it, okay?"

"What is this, a conspiracy between you, mother and father? I'm going to be married and you're all throwing water in my face."

"I'd dump a bucket over your head if I thought it would wake you up."

"What a terrible thing to say. You just don't understand..."

Linda murmured something and turned over on her side with her back to Carrie.

Realizing that her cousin would say no more, Carrie lay back, staring at the ceiling. She had promised her mother she would pray.

Dear God, I don't know what to do. Things are happening so fast and I am so confused. Please, Lord, show me what to do. Don't let me do the wrong thing. Take this burden from me and help me.

She waited for sleep to come, Linda's last words ringing in her head, "You're a little fool."

CHAPTER TWENTY-ONE

SHE WASN'T SURE what awakened her. It was still dark and a warm breeze stirred the curtains at the window. An owl hooted softly somewhere along the riverbank. Rubbing her eyes, she glanced over at Linda's bed, still smarting from her last remark. The bed was empty. Maybe she was in the bathroom. The bathroom was dark and there were no sounds. Puzzled, Carrie got up and opened the bedroom door. There was no light downstairs, so she wasn't in the kitchen.

With a growing sense of apprehension, she slipped on a light robe and her slippers and walked softly down the hall to Andrew's room. If he was sleeping, she just wanted to look at him. If he was awake, well, she wasn't sure what she would do. The door of the guest room was unlatched and swung open silently at her touch. A quick glance around the room told her he wasn't in the bedroom or the bathroom.

She walked softly down the stairs in the darkness. What was she looking for, creeping around like this? Carefully opening the sliding glass door, she stepped out on the porch, listening. Behind the trees, down by the river, she heard the soft murmur of voices. Two people were down by the bench. Was it Andrew and Linda?

Her first thought was to race down there and catch them red-handed. Then, she thought, red-handed at what? She mustn't jump to the wrong conclusion. Maybe they both couldn't sleep and happened to meet outside and walked down to the river together. They could just be talking. She shook her head. Who was she trying to kid? She saw the way they looked at each other at the dinner table.

"I should give them the benefit of the doubt" she murmured to herself. Then Linda's words rang in her head, "You're a fool, Carrie, a fool, a fool—"

The dark blue of her silk robe blended with the shadows as she waited on the porch. Her eyes strained to see beyond the darkness.

Presently she saw a movement and two people walked slowly up the path from the river. Just as Carrie was poised to dash into the house, they paused and turned to each other. In the moonlight there was no mistaking who they were. They appeared deep in conversation. Carrie felt her face flush with anger and humiliation. She was right! Linda was making a play for Andrew right under her nose on the day of the wedding shower.

She watched them walk a few steps and stop to look out over the river. When she saw Andrew turn and take Linda in his arms for a long kiss, she felt she'd seen enough. When they at last neared the house, she slipped inside and dashed up the stairs to her room. She flung off the robe and slipped into bed, waiting. Her heart pounded as she lay there, seething with righteous anger.

Linda opened the door and stepped into the room, closing the door softly behind her. She didn't get into bed but walked over by the window and stood looking out at the moonlight.

"Did you have a nice walk?"

Linda turned abruptly from the window. "I didn't mean to wake you."

"I've been awake long enough."

"Long enough?"

"Long enough to see you come up from the river with Andrew." She tossed the covers back and sat up. "How could you? How could you make a play for my fiancé?" She felt her voice rising.

"Keep your voice down. Do you want to wake the entire household?"

Carrie hissed, "Well, we both know that one other person is already awake, don't we? And don't lie to me, I know everything."

Linda walked slowly over to the bed. "Do you really? I wonder."

"What do you mean? I saw you both clearly in the moonlight."

"That's not what I meant." Linda sat down on the edge of the bed. Her shoulders slumped. "Carrie, don't marry Andrew. It would be the biggest mistake of your life. It wouldn't just ruin your life, it would ruin three others."

Carrie was shocked. "How could my marrying Andrew ruin three lives?"

"Andrew's, Scott's, and mine."

Carrie pressed her fist against her mouth to keep from crying out.

"What are you trying to tell me?"

Linda took a deep breath and let it out slowly. "I'm trying to tell you that Andrew isn't marrying you for love, Carrie. He thought he didn't have a choice. He's not a heel, but he's due to inherit his grandfather's trust fund. He's been letting time go by, and now, he's facing a deadline."

"What are you talking about? What does that have to do with me?"

"Andrew needed a wife, Carrie, before his thirtieth birthday in order to receive the trust."

Carrie gasped. "You're making this up." Then, she looked Linda in the eye, "Is Andrew in love with you?"

Linda paused. "There's something between us, Carrie. I guess you could say something happened the first time we met. I'm not sure Andrew has a drinking problem, but he was frustrated by being forced into a marriage, for the sake of the trust."

Carrie was confused. "But why…"

"Why you? A sweet girl his father could manipulate into marrying Andrew in such a short time. He convinced Andrew that the company was in financial trouble and needed the help. Andrew hadn't realized the stipulation of the trust. His father didn't bring it up because he'd thought Andrew would surely find the right girl before now.

I think his father thought you could balance Andrew out and bring some stability into his life." She got up and went to the window again. "Balance my foot. He steam-rolled over you and you were so starry eyed with that rock on your finger you couldn't see the forest for the trees."

"It's not true. Andrew will…"

"Andrew will tell you everything. He promised me he would do that today."

Carrie could not speak for the lump in her throat. Somehow she knew that Linda was telling the truth and covered her face with her hands.

Linda came over and touched her shoulder. "I'm not as cruel as I seem, Carrie. Perhaps I do love Andrew and feel we might be right for each other. And speaking of right for each other, if you'll take off the rose-colored glasses, you'll see what the rest of the family has known ever since you came home. Scott loves you whether you believe me or not and I think that you will find you love him too. Don't throw a good thing away out of pride. Andrew will marry you if you don't release him. He'll follow his father's wishes."

"I…I have to think."

"You and Andrew need to talk."

"I planned to talk to him, on my own, before all this. You called me a fool. Maybe I am. I wanted—" She burst into tears. Linda reached over to touch her shoulder again but Carrie brushed her hand away. She didn't know who to be the most angry with, Linda or Andrew. All her dreams had turned to dust in a few days.

Linda went over and sat down on the edge of the roll-away bed. Neither spoke for a long time. Carrie looked toward the window where a faint touch of gold proclaimed the coming sunrise.

"Ever since I can remember, you have taken my toys, ordered me about, and walked away with every boy I was interested in. I thought at last I was going to show you all. I had Andrew. He was wealthy, handsome, high society. I was going to be somebody at last. But it's the same pattern. You are still walking away with my best beau. All the glitter, my plans, seem so hollow now, a pile of empty dreams." Carrie laughed softly, but there was no mirth in her voice.

Linda sighed. "I always had to show everyone that I was someone. I talked too much, laughed too much, flirted outrageously. I always had to be the center of attention.

Somehow, in taking away the boys you liked, I proved to myself that I had power. I taught myself to dress well, apply the right makeup, make the right friends—people of influence. Yet I knew that one day you would outshine me, Carrie. You had that gentle nature and beauty that didn't come from bottles and tubes, that natural blond hair that most women would give their eye teeth for. And those blue eyes. You have beautiful eyes. You're a good person, Carrie. You deserve better than what they set up for you. You should be cherished, protected. In Andrew's circles you are sooner or later going to be thrown to the wolves."

It was a long speech for Linda. She had bared her soul and in spite of her hurt, Carrie was touched. She went over and sat down on the rollaway bed. Putting her arms around her cousin, she gave her a hug. Linda hugged her back, and Carrie realized Linda was crying.

"I never meant to deliberately hurt you, Carrie. It was always a game with me. To see how much I could get away with. Now, for the first time in my life, I feel like a real low-life. It's been five years since the affair with Kyle, the married guy. I didn't think any man could get to my heart again. Now, I think I've fallen in love with a man I feel I could spend the rest of my life with, and he turns out to be my own cousin's fiancé."

Carrie had been sitting quietly, listening, and instead of feeling angry and hurt as she had earlier, she felt a peace flow into her heart. She had prayed. Was this God's answer?

"Linda, I think I understand. You know, ever since Andrew and I got engaged I've felt this uneasiness that I couldn't put my finger on. I thought it was just pre-marital jitters, but deep in my heart, I knew it was more than that. Maybe I was fooling myself into thinking I could be happy with Andrew. All the parties, the social whirl, they aren't for me. I was miserable and didn't want to admit it. In giving my heart back to Jesus, I made a commitment. It would never work with Andrew and I think I knew that. Pride and position can never fill the emptiness of being with someone you don't love."

Linda looked up suddenly. "Don't love?"

"No. You were right. I was blinded by money, prestige, all the gifts and pretty things. But my heart isn't as broken as my pride."

"Then, you aren't going to marry Andrew?"

"No. I think we'll all have a nice breakfast, and then I'll take Andrew for a walk."

She looked slyly at her cousin. "Somehow I don't think he'll be heartbroken at my news."

Linda hugged her again, her face alight like a young girl's.

With their arms around each other's shoulders, they sat quietly, watching the dawn come up and contemplating the events of the coming day.

CHAPTER TWENTY-TWO

ANDREW DIDN'T APPEAR for breakfast until almost ten o'clock. He looked rested, but there were dark circles around his eyes. In a casual shirt and slacks, he was once again his charming self. If he had a hangover, he covered it up well. Giving Carrie a perfunctory kiss on the cheek, he didn't look her in the eyes. He and Linda studiously avoided each other, their elaborate casualness making them all the more obvious.

He didn't apologize for the night before because it was too much of a second nature to him. At other house parties he attended, his actions were not an unusual occurrence among guests.

Helen wasn't in any mood to ask Andrew how he liked his eggs and just scrambled them. She added bacon and a homemade apple muffin along with a big glass of orange juice. He looked dubiously at the chunks of green in the eggs as Helen poured him a cup of coffee, tight-lipped and silent. Helen made casual conversation, her face carefully pleasant for Carrie's sake.

"The eggs are wonderful, Mrs. Dickson. I never thought to put avocado in them. You make these often?"

Carrie, feeling surprisingly calm, smiled. "It's an old family favorite."

When they had exhausted the usual mundane conversation, Andrew turned to Carrie. "What time is the shower?"

"At two o'clock."

"Hmmm." He looked at Carrie and chewed on his lip. Linda occupied herself with carefully folding her napkin. She didn't look at them.

He got up and scratched his head. "That was a wonderful breakfast."

Helen softened, barely. "Always like to see our guests well fed."

Andrew strolled into the dining room and walked around the table they had laid the night before. "Looks nice. You girls went to a lot of trouble."

Carrie watched his face. "Linda did all the decorating. She's very good at it."

His eyes met Linda's for the briefest moment before resuming a bland look, but the moment had been long enough.

He loves her. I'm right to let him go, Carrie thought. It would be all wrong. Maybe he loves Linda enough to stop drinking. Maybe she was what he needed. She looked down at her ring and then took Andrew's arm. "Could we take a walk, Andrew? I think you and I have a lot to talk about."

"Sure, babe, we haven't seen each other for a while." He seemed to almost visibly square his shoulders and gave her arm a squeeze. "We do have a lot to talk about."

As they stepped outside, the air had an acrid smell and Carrie wondered why anyone would be burning their fireplace in this heat. The sky was sullen, as though the sun were trying to fight its way past the thin veil of gray clouds.

They walked hand-in-hand toward the steps and were just going to go down the path to the bench when they heard a car race down their driveway spewing gravel.

"Some fool is going too fast for that driveway," Andrew growled.

They hurried back up the steps to see who was in such a hurry. Helen and Linda burst out of the house as Mike, holding his cell phone to his ear, dashed from his shop in the garage and climbed in his CDF truck. Clovis Barnes, the deputy sheriff, jumped out of his patrol car and hurried toward them.

Helen took a step forward. "Clovis, what is it? What's wrong?"

"Fire, ma'am, the whole mountain is ablaze. If it reaches the homes at the top of the hill there's no stopping it! You need to leave, get out of here now. If the fire sweeps down, you won't be able to get across the bridge. "

He turned to Mike, who'd pulled up next to the deputy's car. "They're setting up headquarters in the elementary school, sir."

Mike looked up toward the mountain. "Dear Lord!" he turned to his wife. "Helen, you know what to do. I'll call later when I can. Do what Clovis asks." With a last glance at his family, Mike tore out of the driveway, headed for the CDF station and his fire crew.

Clovis turned to Andrew. "You all need to leave now, sir, orders from the BLM"

Andrew looked around and swore. "I don't see any fire and who is the BLM?"

"Bureau of Land Management, sir."

Carrie knew how hard it was for her dad to leave them, but he knew his job and he would be more help to them directing the fire crews.

Following the direction Clovis pointed, she took off at a dead run for the top of the driveway. As she rounded the curve and got past the large stand of pine trees that hid the mountain from view, she stopped suddenly. With her hand on her heart, she stared with horror at the scene before her.

The entire mountain was on fire and flames were shooting hundreds of feet in the air. The pine trees looked like giant Roman candles as they burst into flame and exploded in the heat.

"Good God!" Andrew had reached her side.

"Oh Andrew, what shall we do?"

"Do? There's nothing you can do. The deputy was right, we need to get out of here now, before we're trapped by the fire!"

"But our house—"

He swore again. "Forget that!" He grabbed her by the arm and began to drag her back toward the house. "Get some things packed, we're all getting out of here, now!"

Carrie broke away and ran toward the porch. "The mountain… it's on fire…huge…we have to leave."

Helen shook her head. "I'm not leaving. We have a perfectly good fire system and we can pump from the river. I'm not giving up without a fight."

Clovis stepped up. "Ma'am, I'd hate to have to arrest you, but orders are orders. If you won't leave, I have to make you leave."

Helen shook her finger in his face. "Clovis, you mean well, and you know we are law-abiding citizens, but you have no authority to make us leave, no matter what the BLM says."

Clovis hesitated, anxiously looking from one to the other. "I'm just doing my job. I don't want to see anyone get hurt."

Helen put her hand on his arm in her usual calming way. "We understand, Clovis, but we aren't leaving our home."

Andrew flung up his hands in exasperation. "This is utter nonsense. I'm not staying around to get burnt to a crisp. I'm getting my things. If you women know what is good for you, you'll do the same and get out of here. No house is worth your life."

A Chevy Blazer raced down the driveway. It was Scott. He jumped out and came over to them.

"I can't do anything about my parent's house. The electricity is cut off and the pump isn't working. They left half an hour ago. I can at least help here. I'll start the pump for the fire system. Andrew, you can help me."

Andrew backed off, his hands in front of him in protest. "Not me, buddy. I'm leaving, and the women are leaving with me. You can't stop a fire that size. It's like pouring a teaspoon of water on a bonfire to put it out." He was clearly frightened.

Scott gave him an even stare. "I guess everyone needs to make up his own mind what to do."

Clovis interrupted. "I was trying to get them to leave, Scott. The BLM says everyone is to get out, fast, and we're running out of time."

Scott turned to the women. "He's right. You can't do anything."

Helen started to protest, but he silenced her with a brief look. "They'll leave," he assured the deputy.

"Okay. Just make it fast. And, thanks, Scott." He got in his car and with another screeching of tires on the gravel, tore up the driveway.

Helen folded her arms. "I am not leaving, Scott."

"Now, Mrs. Dickson, we both know that the fire hose is heavy and when it is full of water it's going to be next to impossible for you to handle it, any of you. I'll stay. All night if I have to, and I'll keep the house watered down. If the fire breaks through and comes down the hill I can always jump in the river."

Andrew took Carrie and Linda by the arm. "Come on. You heard him, we're leaving." He propelled them into the house.

"Carrie, Linda, grab what you need to, we're leaving in five minutes." He hurried down the hall to the guest room.

Linda began throwing clothes in her suitcase. As she was closing it, Carrie came to her side.

"You go with Andrew, Linda. I can't. Mother and I will go to the town hall and wait it out."

"I feel like a rat." Linda searched her face. "Are you sure?"

"Very sure."

They hugged each other tightly.

"Carrie, I'm sorry."

"Don't be. It's all right. God will take care of us. And don't worry about mom. I'll explain it to her, okay?"

Andrew looked totally exasperated as Linda came out and Carrie had obviously not packed anything.

"Where's—" he began.

Carrie put a hand gently on his mouth. "You and Linda go, Andrew." She pulled the ring off her finger and put it in his hand, closing his fingers around it.

"Carrie, what are you doing?"

"The right thing. It never would have worked out with us, Andrew. You two have some things to work out. Take Linda's car and go, now."

He stared at her a moment and as he realized what she was saying, he shook his head in amazement and smiled at her. "You're really something, Carrie. You deserve more than what you got."

She laughed. "Somebody already told me that, I think."

He gave her a brief hug and then put his arm around Linda's shoulders. "You know what you are getting into, Linda?"

She smiled up at him. "I know," she said softly.

Carrie gave them both a gentle push. "Go, now. Get out of here. We'll call and let you know how things are."

Andrew turned back. "Where will you go?"

"To the town hall. It's set up for emergencies. We'll wait out the fire there, and pray."

Andrew and Linda hurried down the stairs and out the door. Helen was helping Scott get the fire hoses out of the boxes on the trees. They turned briefly as Linda's car started up with Andrew at the wheel. Linda ran to her aunt and gave her a brief hug.
"Carrie will explain. I'm sorry. Please call me at my apartment and tell me how you are. You are going, aren't you?"

Helen opened her mouth but no words came out. She shut it again abruptly, nodded, and stared as Linda ran back to the car and got in. They drove quickly up the driveway and out of sight. Scott uncoiled the hose and hooked it up to the pump. The generator hummed as he too stood and looked after the retreating car. He watched Linda and Andrew drive away then turned to Carrie, one eyebrow cocked, but there was no time for questions.

"Mother, we'd better go too. We can't help Scott here. Get what you can pick up in a couple of minutes."

"You ladies better get a move on," Scott urged them, "The Lord and I will take care of your house."

Helen sighed. "You're right, Scott. Prayer is the only thing that will help now." She turned to her daughter. "We'll need to take the cars out. We'll each drive our own. I'll take Nubbins in the Bronco."

As they rushed into the house, Carrie looked briefly at the living room and the dining room, all decorated for the shower. She bowed her head briefly. "Lord, I know this is all going to work out. It's all in Your hands. There's nothing we can do but pray." She hurried upstairs.

Looking around her room, she wondered what to take. All her life was in this room, this house. What do you pack in a matter of minutes? A peace came over her and with a smile she grabbed a change of clothes and her Bible. Without a backward glance, she hurried out the door.

When they got up on the main road where they could see the houses and the fire, people had stopped all along the road to watch. Some women had tears in their eyes. The men tried to look stoic as they watched the red and orange monster gobble up the forest. Over their heads two giant helicopters with thousand-gallon buckets suspended on cables, roared toward the fire. The people on the road watched as the crafts hovered over the flames and emptied their loads before heading back to the deep holes in the river where they could refill their buckets.

Aerial bombers droned overhead, dumping their loads of boron into the heart of the fire.

One man was listening to a radio and announced to everybody nearby, "We're the only big fire going in the whole state right now, looks like we get the whole shebang. Fire crews comin' from all over. Help's on the way, folks!"

Everyone cheered until one older woman looked back at the fire and asked wistfully, "but will they be in time?"

Carrie, her mother, and their neighbors the Merritts, gathered in a circle and began to pray earnestly for God to spare their homes. They prayed for several heartfelt moments. But were interrupted as a cheer went up.

"Look!" someone shouted.

The wind had come up, and the blaze that had almost reached the homes at the top sector of Pine Flat, was slowly turning northward to an uninhabited area. People hugged and cried. The wind could turn the fire again, but for the moment their homes had been spared.

At the urging of the deputies who were patrolling the street, people got back in their cars. They needed to clear the street for the fire vehicles and crews coming in. Reluctantly, the motley parade of cars, trucks, and campers made their way toward the town hall. Carrie could see the roof of their house partially hidden in the trees. Would it still be there tomorrow? She thought of Scott, unable to protect his own home yet risking his life to save theirs.

Protect him, Lord. Keep him safe. I have so much to tell him.

CHAPTER TWENTY-THREE

CARRIE PARKED THE Mustang, made sure the canvas top was securely fastened down, and waited for her mother to arrive. When Helen got there they tied Nubbins to a tree and put his water bowl next to him. He lay down obediently, but his eyes followed their every movement.

People stood around talking quietly. The smell of fresh coffee wafted out around them and many headed up the steps into the hall to get a cup. The local grocery store had brought out its whole stock of fruit, donuts, cupcakes, and other snack food. Volunteers were piling them on a long table so people could help themselves. On the steps, on the grass, in small circles of chairs inside, people stood or sat. No one knew what to do next. Carrie felt like she was in a huge hospital waiting room where the family members waited to hear news, good or bad, about a loved one. They could all handle the news, they thought, but it was the waiting that was so hard.

Jeff Merritt scratched his head. "Shoot, what are you goin' to take from a house you've lived in thirty years, on such short notice?"

Jean Merritt put a hand on his shoulder. "Well, we got the family pictures, Jeff. Those can't be replaced."

He got up and walked a short distance away, not looking at them.

"Jeff practically built that house himself. He's put so much into it. I know we could build another house, but we're older now, and it wouldn't be the same."

Helen put her hand over Jean's. "I think we all feel the same way. We get used to our special things around us. Things we treasure because we've gathered them over the years or received them as heirlooms from our families. It's hard to turn these things over to the Lord and let go. We have to trust Him through this."

"I know. It's one thing to talk about trusting and another thing to do it." Jean looked over at Carrie. "This must be hard on you, honey, having all this happen the day of your wedding shower. By the way, where's your fiancé? Didn't he make it up here? They may not let him through at this point."

"I got hold of him. He'll stay in the Bay Area for now." It was mostly the truth.

"Well, you were fortunate to have reached him before he got in all this mess. Guess you'll have to postpone the shower."

"Yes, that's true."

Carrie just smiled and turned to watch the street in front of the town hall. The buses and large green trucks from the forestry service and honor camps continued to roll by. The faces of the men in the windows were grim. Most of them would be working with an axe or shovel, digging trenches along the fire lines and spreading dirt on the flames in hopes of containing the fire. Others would be using their shovels to beat out hot spots and small fires spread by the mother flames. They would be fighting the heat of the summer along with the incredible inferno of the fire lines. It was like facing all the forces of hell.

Many of the men in their community would be on the fire lines. She wondered if Scott would eventually join the fire crews when their house was safe, or when there was nothing more he could do there.

As she looked down at the tree where Nubbins was tied, she saw her mother walk over to the family pet. She sat down on the grass, absentmindedly stroking the dog's head as she stared down the road Andrew and Linda had taken a short time earlier.

Carrie went over and joined her, putting her hand over her mother's. "They'll be all right."

"Linda and Andrew? What in the world happened, Carrie? What's going on?"

"Andrew wasn't in love with me, Mother. There was a bigger picture and I didn't see it."

Helen's lips tightened. "I know she's my niece, but she's always done this to you, Carrie. Don't you think I saw what was happening? You should have put up a fight. Andrew was your fiancé." She finally turned and looked at her daughter.

"I can't say I'm sad that you aren't going to marry that young man, he has problems, but now I worry about Linda."

Carrie laughed with a lightness she hadn't felt in a long time. "I don't think Andrew's drinking problem is serious. Linda can handle him."

Helen sighed. "So what you're telling me is that Andrew and Linda are better matched?"

Relieved at her mother's perception of the situation, Carrie nodded. "I think Andrew will be a challenge for Linda, but not one she can't handle." She gave her mother a sly grin. "She can also deal with Andrew's father. He won't intimidate her like he could me."

"Intimidate?"

"Oh Mother, Linda saw it all. She said they were steam-rolling me into marriage because Andrew's father thought I would be easy to manipulate, and I was. Andrew confided to her that he has to marry before he is thirty to inherit his grandfather's trust. He didn't love me, but he was going along with his father's wishes, thinking he has to save the company. I guess there were some problems."

Her mother stared at her, trying to take in all Carrie was saying. "So what will happen now?"

"Don't be upset, but it's my guess Linda will take my place at the wedding I didn't have any say in planning." Carrie grinned at her mother. "She knows what she's getting into."

Helen flung up one hand. "Just a slight change, the bride's cousin for the bride. I just don't know what to think right now." She turned to Carrie, searching her face.

"You're not hurt over this, dear? You seem almost cheerful."

"I didn't love Andrew, Mother, though I didn't realize it until this last week. God has been trying to tell me all along but I wouldn't listen. I loved all the gifts and the parties and the attention. No one has ever treated me like that. I was blinded, as Linda pointed out, by that huge ring on my finger."

Her mother looked down at Carrie's left hand. "You gave it back."

"Yes, before they left. Andrew understood. I couldn't keep it, not now."

"I prayed so hard that you would make the right choice. I didn't feel Andrew was right for you. That was so clear last night, but it had to be your decision. You know I would have loved Andrew, if he was your choice. I don't think ill of him."

"I know, Mother. I'm so thankful you didn't try to persuade me or talk me out of it. I needed to sort things out for myself."

Helen smiled and reached out with a big hug. "I think we need to pray. Andrew and Linda will need all the help they can get—your father, too. We don't know what he'll be up against with this fire. It's the biggest one we've had in years. "

Later, as they sat quietly watching the fire crews continue to come in, Carrie noticed some small trailers being unhitched on the grass by the pavilion. The Forestry Department took over that area as their outdoor kitchen to feed the crews. The sides of the trailers were let down to reveal double sinks with soap dispensers on each side. She marveled at how efficient the whole process was. The elementary school became headquarters to direct the firefighters and equipment. The parking lot of the Community Church was filled with red California Department of Forestry trucks with CDF in large letters on the doors.

A huge semi lumbered onto the church parking lot and when one side was dropped down, a mobile laundry was revealed with commercial washers and dryers.

Later in the afternoon, a truck pulled up in front of the hall and two men got out. Right behind them a station wagon pulled up and four people jumped out—a woman and three men. They began to unload cots, blankets, and pillows from the back of the truck. Some of the men standing around went over to help, grateful for something constructive to do. Soon the main room of the hall looked like a giant dormitory with the rows of cots.

The woman seemed to be in charge, and Carrie found out she was from the Red Cross. She gathered everyone around and assured them that food was on the way. The Red Cross needed to have an estimate of how many box suppers to pack. She got a general head count and dashed away in the station wagon again.

By ten o'clock that evening, the food still hadn't come and people were going to the local hamburger stand and the Lewiston Café. The two restaurants, not supplied for such a huge deluge of customers, soon ran out of food. More provisions wouldn't arrive until the next day.

Finally, a little after midnight, another truck arrived from the Red Cross and volunteers began to unload crates of box suppers. A 'T' or 'H' on the box indicated turkey or ham sandwiches. Each box also contained an apple or an orange, a small container of potato salad, a bag of chips and a package of cookies. It wasn't an exciting dinner, but people were hungry. Carrie chose a turkey sandwich.

She and her mother sat on the steps again, since the air was still warm and it was stuffy inside the hall. Few people could sleep and most just sat and watched the activity going on around them.

"I wonder how Daddy's doing with his fire crews."

Helen leaned up against the railing. "I worry about him, but it doesn't do any good. He has to do his job."

A Highway Patrol car pulled up about one o'clock in the morning and the officer had a short conference with a couple of men from the forestry office. Carrie gathered her courage and went over to talk to them.

"Excuse me, but can you tell me anything about Pine Flat? Is the fire still going the other way?"

The officer looked at some notes. "Pine Flat is still okay but not out of danger if the fire turns again. We'll know more later this morning. We did arrest some guy there who wasn't supposed to be in the area. Lots of empty homes, unguarded, you know."

"A man arrested?" She thought of Scott. Did they think he was trespassing at their home? "Do you know his name?"

"Can't give that out, ma'am."

"Oh. Well, thank you anyway. At least my mother will be relieved that our home is still okay."

"Yes, ma'am." The officer nodded politely and she remembered she had interrupted their conversation. She hurried away to tell her mother the good news about their house and the man who was arrested.

By two o'clock, Carrie was getting sleepy and she saw that her mother was exhausted.

"Why don't we go in and rest awhile? They'll let us know if there is any more news. The officer said they'll have information later this morning."

"I don't think I mind even sleeping on a canvas cot at this point. I'm beat." Helen stood up and stretched. They put Nubbins in the back of the Bronco with his bowl of water.

In the hall they were surprised by how few people were taking advantage of the cots. Finding a quiet corner, they picked out cots and settled themselves for sleep. Carrie thought the ticking of the big clock on the wall would keep her awake, but it was the last thing she remembered.

Five hours later, stiff, and her mouth tasting like it was full of cotton, Carrie sat up. Her mother still slept. She got up, folded the blanket, and went in search of some coffee. The volunteers had done their job, keeping the pot going. She eyed the powdered cream with distaste, but put in several heaping spoonfuls and added a packet of sugar for some energy. Most of the snack things were gone and what was left looked picked over. She went to the Bronco and let Nubbins out for a walk.

The town took on a carnival look with all the activity and people rushing here and there. Over by the pavilion, firefighters lined up four deep for two blocks waiting to get some breakfast. They were dirty and most looked almost too weary to stand in line. Carrie began to feel a sense of the enormity of the whole fire-fighting process. People, food, equipment, vehicles, all appearing within hours and more pouring in. A bus went by with the name of an Oregon church on it, full of more men to fight the fire. No doubt they'd ridden all night to get here. They unloaded and lined up at the registration booth. Their names, addresses, and experience were noted and they were given their assignments. Trucks lined up to take each group off as soon as they were processed.

Though dead tired, the men in the breakfast line gave her appreciative smiles as she approached. Evidently she did not appear as grubby as she felt. She stopped by one young man, who bent down and scratched Nubbins' ears. He seemed friendly.

"How long have you been fighting this fire?"

"Came in yesterday morning, about sixteen hours I reckon."

"Sixteen hours? Is that a normal shift?"

Someone guffawed. "Ma'am, you work until you get a replacement. That fire doesn't take a break and we don't get one either."

"Oh. I'm sorry. I didn't understand that. We do appreciate all you are doing, so much. I want to thank whoever saved our area of homes."

"Where do you live, miss." This from a tall, black man with smudges on his face.

"Pine Flat."

The men shuffled ahead as the line moved, and Carrie moved with them.

"Pine Flat? I worked near there at the beginning of the fire. We didn't save your house, ma'am."

She sucked in her breath quickly, her eyes wide with alarm. "You mean that area burned down?"

"No ma'am, not that, I mean that we can't take credit for saving your homes over there. If the wind hadn't come up when it did and turned the fire in another direction, into the back hills, there was nothing we could have done. We just couldn't get into place fast enough to stop that fire."

She let her breath out with a big sigh of relief. "Then our house is still there. Well thank you anyway, all of you, for your hard work. God must have heard our prayers if the fire hasn't turned back."

"Amen," said the black man.

Several of the men had been petting Nubbins and he had enjoyed the attention, but now he strained at the leash, anxious to be moving along.

She waved at the firemen and headed back to the town hall just as the Red Cross truck pulled up again, this time loaded with boxed breakfasts.

Lines formed quickly. Carrie tied Nubbins to the tree and went into the hall. Her mother was awake.

"There you are. I wondered where you went."

"I took Nubbins for a walk."

"Never thought I'd see the day I would sleep without washing my face," Helen muttered.

Carrie took Helen's arm. "Breakfast is served, ma'am, such as it is."

A sweet roll, fruit again, a container of juice, and a box of cereal was the morning offering. Containers of milk were on the table for those who wanted cereal.

Helen opted for the coffee first. Just as they were all settling on the steps, a CDF truck stopped in front of the hall and a man with a megaphone got out.

"Folks, can I have your attention, please? We have some information."

Everyone fixed their eyes on him and lapsed into an expectant silence.

"The fire is moving down the canyon toward the old highway. If it continues on that course, it may threaten some homes there, but we may be able to contain it at the junction."

Questions were fired from the crowd. "How long will that be?"

"Maybe by tomorrow. Can't say. It's a pretty tough fire."

"How much has it burned? Any more houses?"

"One house and a cabin. Fire's consumed over two thousand acres so far. It's throwing out flames half a mile ahead of itself. The aerial bombers are doing their best to keep a steady flow of chemicals and the water carriers are protecting the crews in the most dangerous area."

"How many men on the fire lines?"

"Close to a thousand right now. We could use more if we had them. More coming in today."

"How soon can we return to our homes?"

"Coming to that. I have a list of tentative safe areas I'll read off. You can go back around eleven today."

People clapped and cheered.

As he read off the names of streets and areas they held their breath. When he called out, "Pine Flat," the two women hugged each other.

"Folks, remember that this is tentative. If there is any change in the fire, you may have to leave again, understood?"

Everyone nodded or murmured assent.

Carrie approached the man with the megaphone. "Can you tell me where Mike Dickson is working? I'm his daughter, Carrie."

"Your dad's supervising the base camp, Carrie. He's okay." He gave her a brief smile and climbed back into his truck.

Carrie looked at her breakfast box and left the fruit. "You know, Mother, I never realized how much I appreciated your wonderful breakfasts."

Helen finished up the last of her coffee. "Tell you what. Tomorrow morning we'll do it up right. I'd feed Scott every morning for as long as he wants for looking after our house like that."

She looked toward the gray clouds of smoke that rose above the mountain, obscuring the sun. "I do hope he's all right. He must be exhausted."

Carrie had been thinking of Scott. Did he really return her feelings? Was Linda right? Was he in love with her as Linda said? What should she say or do when they got back home? What did he think when he saw Linda leaving with Andrew? Her mind whirled with questions. There was really nothing she could do except wait until she saw him again. She hoped he wasn't the man arrested, but then she couldn't picture the deputy arresting Scott Spencer. Everyone knew what kind of man he was. *As I do.* She watched the strange, smoky clouds for a long time.

The Spencers hadn't appeared at the town hall and Helen found out they'd unhooked the motor home and driven it out to the home of friends in Weaverville. She had wanted to tell them about Scott, but perhaps he'd already told them what he was going to do.

It seemed an eternity until eleven A.M. but people finally piled into their vehicles and started in the direction of their homes. Helen led the way with Carrie following. As they approached the street leading to their road, they were stopped by a roadblock. *Now what's wrong?*

An officer approached her car.

"Name, ma'am?"

"Carrie Dickson."

"I.D. Please."

She showed him her driver's license as he scanned a sheet in front of him. "Pine Flat?"

"Yes, sir."

"You may proceed. Remember this is only tentative. Tune in your radio for any new bulletins on the fire."

"Yes, sir." She moved ahead.

As they crossed the bridge, Carrie looked over and saw their house through the trees. Tears slipped down her cheeks as she thought of how close they had come to losing it.

"Thank You, Lord. Thank You for our home, for giving it back to us."

They approached their driveway and saw a water truck parked alongside the meadow that separated their house from the neighbors. Firefighters were sprawled on the grass, resting or sleeping. Another plane passed overhead, on its way to the front lines.

As they neared the house, Carrie felt a stab of disappointment. The Blazer was gone. The hoses were laid out to drain, but ready if they were needed again. Then she saw the note on the back door.

Deputies patrolling the area but locked the house up just in case. One man arrested casing a house, non-resident. Everything ok. They need more men on the fire lines so I'll be back when I can.

Scott

CHAPTER TWENTY-FOUR

$\mathcal{H}$ELEN WENT TO check the kitchen and found a cup and plate in the sink. Scott had at least eaten a little something. She poured out the remains of cold coffee and set about straightening up. The message button on the answering machine was flashing and Carrie pushed it.

There were numerous messages. Many people were praying for them and apologizing for having to leave the area, most hoping the shower would be re-scheduled after the fire. Helen stood with her and listened. "Now that our home is safe, I'll just call the list and tell them the shower is off. That is, if it is all right with you, dear."

"I can help call, Mother. It's partly my doing and I might as well face up to it."

"Are you sure?"

Carrie nodded and gave her mother a hug. "What do you say we get these decorations put away?"

They worked quickly, folding and stowing things away. In a short time they looked around and there was no longer anything to indicate a bridal shower had almost taken place.

"At least we didn't have the napkins engraved," Carrie murmured as she put the last package in a drawer. They returned to the kitchen.

Helen shook her head slowly, "I have no idea what I'm going to do with that cake. Maybe the Spencers can serve it at their barbeque in July."

"That's a great idea, Mom. When Nola finds out what happened, I'm sure she'd be glad to help you get rid of it. Half the county comes to their barbeque."

Carrie picked up some lemons from a bowl and began to squeeze lemon juice and made some lemonade while her mother made egg salad sandwiches.

As she savored her sandwich and a dish of home canned peaches, Carrie thought lunch had never tasted so good.

Her mother took the first shift of phone calls, so Carrie went out on the porch to watch one of the helicopters churn its way past their house. It was enormous, the size of three regular helicopters. The water buckets, each holding a thousand gallons, had to be terribly heavy. The brush along the river was flattened by the force of the wind created by the whirling blades where the helicopters hovered to refill the bucket.

Looking toward the river where she had seen Linda and Andrew together, it was hard to imagine that it was only a day ago. She thought with chagrin of the scene that must have taken place with Dietrich Van Zant and with a twinge of guilt, was glad she didn't have to face him. "You're braver than I am, Linda," she murmured to herself.

Trying to picture Linda in the beautiful wedding dress, she shook her head. It wasn't her cousin's style and neither was the big church wedding. She let her imagination wander and saw Linda in a tea-length dress, in a garden setting. Andrew was smiling, his hair rumpled as he looked at her. Then, the groom's hair wasn't auburn anymore, and a face superimposed itself over Andrew's. She saw the dark hair and the deep-set blue eyes that pierced her heart. She reached out her hand as she came toward him and Scott grasped it with his own.

She sat quietly, as the scene faded, letting the sweet, cleansing pain of love permeate her being. God had kept her from making a terrible mistake. She would wait and trust Him to bring whatever He planned for her and Scott.

That evening, Carrie took her turn phoning the women on the bridal shower list. They didn't dwell on details, but only said what they had agreed on. That there had been a change in plans and the wedding had been called off. There was no need to feed the gossip machine any more than necessary. Carrie's wedding and engagement ring had been the talk of the community before the fire, and now when the news of the fire began to fade, no doubt the broken engagement and cancelled wedding would be news again.

Carrie called the Spencers, but got their answering machine. She hoped to be able to ask about news of Scott but that would have to wait.

The rollaway bed was folded up and Carrie and her mother hefted it downstairs to the porch so Olen Ferguson could pick it up. There were still firefighters on the meadow and trucks parked on the dry grass at the head of the property. Water trucks made their way up the road several times a day. Scott wasn't with this particular crew or their replacements. This crew was doing the mop-up operation, keeping an eye on hot spots—areas that were still smoldering and could again burst into flame.

One firefighter told Carrie about some strange holes with tunnels going off in several directions. It turned out that they were left from some huge pine trees. The fire leaped into the branches, and soon the whole tree was on fire. The intense heat had burned up the tree and traveled down into the ground to consume even the roots. Ancient majestic pines had disappeared in moments, leaving only the strange holes in the ground to mark their passing.

There was word that the logging crew working up on the mountain was going to be charged with starting the fire, but Helen was of the opinion that nothing would really come of it.

"Mark my words; they'll be doing the salvage operation as though they had nothing to do with creating the salvage!"

Carrie decided to go to the post office for the mail. She went through the check point and waved to the officer. As she passed their church parking lot she noticed that another booth had gone up. They were silk screening T-shirts that said "Pine Top Fire" with the month and year. She stopped the car and got out, curious that anyone would have the gall to make T-shirts to mark such a serious occasion.

"Don't you think these are inappropriate? There are a lot of men working on this fire that are risking their lives and you're making T-shirts?"

The man in the booth was unperturbed. "Lady, the firefighters themselves call us and tell us where the fire is and ask us to come."

"They do? But, why?"

"They're risking their lives and they want a memento of their efforts, to mark a brief moment of glory, if you like. They buy the T-shirts, hats, and whatever else"

Carrie was amazed. "That's really something. I never would have thought of it." She picked out a light blue T-shirt and watched while the man whirled the wheel with the different colors of silk screen paint. In no time her shirt was done and the colors dried. Perhaps if Scott didn't have one, it would be a way to say thank you.

She saw that the registration booth was temporarily quiet and wandered over. A man in uniform looked up expectantly.

"Excuse me. We have a neighbor's son who is working on the fire lines. Do you suppose you could tell me what area he is working in? I'd like to tell his folks."

"I was thinking you were a little lightweight to volunteer, though we have quite a few women on the lines."

"There are women on the fire lines?"

"That's right. They work as hard as the men do. Of course we try to place them in less dangerous areas unless they are experienced firefighters. Now who were you looking for?"

"His name is Scott Spencer."

"Oh, young Scott. I know him. He's been on lookout duty with us a couple of summers." He ran his finger down a page of names and then started on the next page. "We'll get a computer print-out shortly, but the names are listed as they signed up."

"He would have signed up day before yesterday, around noon."

"Scott, Scott, ah, yes, here he is. Up on the ridge."

CHAPTER TWENTY-FOUR

"Is that a dangerous area of the fire?" She held her breath.

"I'm afraid it is today." He looked up toward the mountain. "It's right in the heart of the fire."

She didn't want him to see how upset she was. After quickly thanking him for the information, she hurried back to the car.

God, please watch over Scott and the other men with him. Keep them from harm and bring them back safely to their families. Please help them put the fire out soon."

She drove up to the hill behind the post office and looked toward the mountains. Angry orange flames shot hundreds of feet into the air. Ponderous clouds of heavy gray smoke billowed ominously into the sky. As she watched, the flames seemed to grow even bigger in defiance of the tiny creatures that battled it—like a huge dragon, laughing at the small knights in armor who sought to bring it down.

As she turned down the driveway, she saw the Chevy Blazer parked by the house. Hopefully, she hurried into the house. Nola and Allen Spencer were having a cup of coffee with her mother. No Scott.

"Mr. and Mrs. Spencer, I'm glad you're here."

"Carrie. We are so sorry to hear the engagement is called off. I'm sure it is for the best, but it is difficult, I know." Nola Spencer gave Carrie one of her kind smiles. "You know I was engaged to someone else when I met this bushy giant." She gave her husband a fond look. "He didn't have a beard then, though."

"You broke your engagement?"

"Yes, I did. I knew Allen was the right man for me."

Her husband tried to shrug it off. "Well, the best man usually wins out, doesn't he?"

Nola swatted him on the shoulder.

"Mr. and Mrs. Spencer, I have some news of Scott."

"Do you know where he is?"

"Yes, up on the ridge. I asked at the sign-up booth. I thought you might want to know."

Allan Spencer fixed her with those eyes that were so like Scott's. "Do you happen to know where that is in relation to the fire?"

She hadn't wanted to share that part, but there was no getting around it. "It's pretty close to the main fire."

Helen went over to the television and switched it on. The midday news was on. There were the usual political items, and, then, the camera switched to scenes of the fire. The announcer spoke in ominous tones.

"—Brown's Mountain Fire which has been burning for three days. Fire crews from many states have been battling the flames. So far it is contained on the south and west perimeter. Firefighters on the north perimeter are in such intense heat that they are replacing them in two-hour shifts. There has been one casualty...a heart attack that occurred on the fire line. The name is being withheld until family is notified. This is a big one, folks. We will now switch to John Summerfield, who has been covering the fire."

The camera switched to a reporter in yellow slickers. Behind him were various pieces of fire equipment, men moving about, and several tents. An ambulance was in the background.

"Good afternoon, I'm at a command post at the base of the mountains where the fire has resisted the crew's efforts for fourteen hours. They are trying to bring in firefighters from other areas to help. The men are exhausted. One man suffered a heart attack while fighting the fire, and men risked their own lives to bring him down."

As the camera panned the fires, showing the intense flames, they could hear the crackling of the fire in the background. Zooming in on the faces of some of the men who were sitting on the ground, the camera caught them in various stages of exhaustion, resting from their stint against the blaze.

Everyone in their living room strained to try to see Scott among them. The firefighters were so covered with grime and soot it was hard to tell. Maybe he was out of camera range. Switching back to John Summerfield, he was about to sign off when someone handed him a note.

"Folks, we have a bulletin here. There is a group of firefighters trapped in a canyon. They are cut off by the fire from escape. Another crew is battling their way up the left flank to try to get to them. The flames and smoke are so high the helicopters can't get close enough to release the water from the carriers. This is serious, folks. If that crew can't reach them they may not make it. It's going to take a miracle to get them out. We'll keep you posted on the situation. Now, back to the station, this is John Summerfield for Channel Six news."

The small group looked at each other in dismay. Was Scott in that group trapped in the canyon? One by one they slipped to their knees and joined hands as they prayed earnestly for Scott and the men with him.

A tear slipped out and rolled down Carrie's face as they once again stood. Nola gave her a questioning look, and then, with gradual understanding, she put her arm around Carrie's shoulders.

"Scott is in the best possible hands, dear. I think in every way."

The next news wouldn't be until five o'clock, but the station promised to interrupt with any late-breaking news of the fire. Carrie stayed in the living room after the Spencers left. She didn't want to miss a single bulletin.

CHAPTER TWENTY-FIVE

CLOSE TO THREE o'clock, the program Carrie was watching was suddenly cut off and the screen switched to the newsroom. She leaned forward on the edge of her chair and called out, "Mother, I think there's another bulletin about the fire."

Helen rushed in from the kitchen just as the newscaster was finishing his update on the spread of the fire. There was a lot of noise in the background and the camera focused on John Summerfield's face.

"…We've been tracking the efforts of the firefighters here to reach the men trapped in that canyon. A little while ago the chief told me that the crew that was struggling to reach them had just returned to camp. They were beaten back by the flames. Our hearts go out to the families of those brave men whom we have lost to this epic fire—"

Carrie put her hand over her mouth and gasped. Her mother clasped her hands together.

"Oh, dear God." She turned to Carrie. "I talked to Nola a little while ago. They got word from a friend on the forestry crew an hour ago. Scott is in that crew. He's one of the men trapped by the fire!"

"Oh Mother, I don't want Scott to die. I love him. I wanted to tell him when the fire was over. Now I'll never be able to…" Tears coursed down her cheeks.

Helen put her arms around Carrie and gently patted her back. "Oh, darling, I thought that's how it was."

Helen turned toward the television with a determined look on her face. "It's not over until they tell us they are dead and bring the bodies down. Where is our faith? We need to just keep praying for that boy and those with him. That announcer said it would take a miracle. Well, haven't we got a miracle-working God?" Her eyes flashed with righteous indignation.

John Summerfield was talking with one of the firefighters who had tried to reach the trapped men. Feeling a bit chastened by her mother's words, Carrie turned to listen.

"We're talking with Evan Masters, one of the men on the rescue crew. They've just come down from the mountain. Tell us, Evan, what was it like up there?"

The camera moved in for a close-up on a man's face. He looked haggard and his eyes were like white holes in a face covered with soot.

"It was terrible. The heat—couldn't get to them. We tried several ways and the flames beat us back. We were almost trapped ourselves. One of our men is burned pretty bad. Oh God! My boy is up there. I tried to reach him. Mary, I tried to reach Joe—" the man looked straight at the camera, struggling with his emotions. Finally he put a hand over his eyes and his shoulders shook. "We just couldn't reach them. We couldn't make it…" He turned away from the camera and another firefighter put his arm around the man's shoulders and led him away.

"Oh, Mother, that poor man. He was trying to save his son."

Helen nodded, tears in her eyes.

When John Summerfield turned back to the camera his eyes appeared moist.

"That was Evan Masters. He was pretty overcome, folks. His son is on that trapped crew. To say that emotions are running pretty high here is an understatement. I have the Chief of Operations here. Chief, how do you see the chances of those men who are trapped up there?"

Both women leaned toward the television. It was Mike. His face looked haggard, and tired.

"We've done all we could. Every route we've tried to reach them is blocked off by the fire. My heart goes out to the families of those brave men who've given the ultimate sacrifice in the line of duty. Believe me, as soon as the fire has moved on, we'll be heading to, ah, recover them."

"Thank you for those compassionate words, Chief. And now, back to the studio and…"

Suddenly he was interrupted by cheering in the background. The whole camp had gone wild. Men who had been sprawled, exhausted, on the ground got up and were waving their hands in the air and hugging one another.

"Folks, stay with us, there seems to be something happening." The reporter turned to the crowd. One man clapped him on the shoulder and put his face in front of the camera.

"The trapped crew! They just stumbled into camp. They're here, alive! They made it out! Yee haw!"

The two women jumped up and down and hugged one another as they watched the commotion on the television. Helen grabbed the phone to call the Spencers but it was busy. No matter. They were sure to be watching the news themselves.

John Summerfield beckoned to his camera crew and they worked their way through the jubilant crowd of firefighters to a small group of men who looked like they had been through the end of the world. Their clothes were singed and they looked ready to drop at any moment.

"Can one of you tell us what happened?" The reporter was looking for someone to put his mike in front of.

"Ask Scott. He can tell you what happened," one of the men said slowly, shaking his head from side to side. "I don't think I could explain it if I tried."

A man Carrie barely recognized was urged forward and the crowd hushed to listen.

"Your name, sir?"

"Scott Spencer."

"Can you tell us what happened up there? We thought you weren't going to make it."

Mike Dickson came and stood next to Scott as he began to speak. "We were working the area assigned to us when we were cut off from the rest of the crew by a huge burning tree that fell. It was like thunder when it hit the ground. We looked for an escape route, and thought we were headed in the right direction, but there were flames all around us and we got disoriented. There seemed no way to go. We tried to find shelter but there was nothing. We were out in the open and not sure our heat shields would work. The ground was too hard to dig ourselves down into. If that one firefighter hadn't made it up to us and showed us the way out, we'd be dead for sure." He turned to Mike. "I'd sure like to thank him, Mr. Dickson, he saved our lives."

John Summerfield put his mike in front of Carrie's father. "Somebody got to them after all, Chief. Any idea who it was?"

Mike ignored the reporter, staring somberly at Scott for a long moment in amazement. "Scott, I'd like to take credit for a rescue crew, but I can't. The group of men we sent couldn't make it anywhere near you. They had to return to camp."

"But one of them couldn't have. We were praying and waiting for the end to come, hoping it would be quick, when this big firefighter stepped through what seemed like an impassable wall of fire and shouted at us to follow him. We figured that if he made it through, we could too. We grabbed our gear and ran toward him. We had to go through some fire, but it was only a short distance. We got a little singed but made it to another clearing. There was a small granite overhang, a kind of indentation in the rock like a cave. The big guy pointed to that and told us to squeeze in as far back as we could. It was just big enough for the eight of us. We tucked our heat shields around us and waited. Just then the fire leaped over our hiding place and roared past us. I looked for the man who led us to safety thinking he had squeezed in with us, but he'd disappeared. I hoped he'd made it back to camp, maybe another way. When we felt it was safe, we got out of there and came down the side of the mountain opposite the fire."

Mike put a large hand on Scott's shoulder. "Son, all of the men sent to rescue you came back, all of them. None of them were able to reach you. I have no idea who that firefighter was."

Scott stared at him a moment in disbelief and then looked down at his feet, shaking his head. When he looked up at the camera again, there were tears in his eyes.

"We were praying and asking God to help us and get us out of there. If that man wasn't on the fire crew, then he had to be one of God's angels. Without him we wouldn't be here."

Mike enveloped Scott in a bear hug and shook his head. "Thank God, son, thank God."

John Summerfield for once was speechless. Everyone listening was overcome with the enormity of what they had just heard.

Finally, the reporter looked into the camera. "Folks, we've just heard an astounding story. If I weren't here, seeing it happen, I'm not sure I would believe it myself. We have no other explanation for the rescue of these men. You heard the Chief say none of the rescue crew was able to reach these men. It's truly a miracle. Whether it was an angel or not, we sure don't know, but what we do know is that these men were trapped, given up for lost, and now they stand in front of us, alive, rescued from a terrible death in a fiery inferno. This "miracle on the mountain" is a story these men will be telling their children in the years to come. And now, back to our local station. This is John Sumerfield at the base camp, Brown's Mountain Fire."

The phone rang and when Helen answered it she was jubilant.

"Yes, Nola we were watching. Yes, praise God, a wonderful miracle. We are so happy for you both. God heard our prayers. Yes, of course. Let us know. Our love to Allen, too."

She hung up and beamed at them. "They saw the newscast and just wanted to share the news. They are so relieved and thankful. They'll let us know if they have any more news from Scott."

The phone rang again and Helen picked it up. She listened for a moment and her face told Carrie who it was.

"Yes dear. We are all fine. The house is fine. Yes, we saw the news. You were watching? Well, then, you know Scott and his crew weren't saved by a rescue team. Yes, it is truly a miracle."

Helen listened again and then asked quietly, "Are you all right?" She nodded at the phone. "Yes, Carrie explained it to us. I'm not sure I understand it all, but I'll pray for you and Andrew." She paused and her eyes got big as she glanced back at her daughter.

"He did? Well, I guess it will be all right. This is all so fast you have my head spinning. What are we to do? I understand. Maybe that is better. You're going ahead with it, then? We just need to trust the Lord for the outcome of all this. You have my love, Linda, you know that, and no, we're not angry with Andrew. Yes, Carrie knows that. God's hand must be in all of this and we just have to trust Him. Yes, I will. I love you too, Linda."

She hung up the phone slowly and turned to face Carrie.

"Andrew's father was a bit shocked at the outcome, but when they told him that Carrie had broken the engagement and given him his ring back, with the time frame, he had no choice but to agree to the wedding. He and Andrew had a long talk and they are going through with everything. It won't be at the La Jolla church, though. Linda convinced him that under the circumstances, it would be better to have a smaller affair, in the garden."

My dream, Carrie thought, *just like my dream*. She knew Linda would have her way. Carrie could only stare at her mother.

"They still plan on July Fourth." Now Helen looked hesitant. "She wants your father and me to come. Under the circumstances there is no need for you to go, Carrie. It would be difficult. Linda understands that."

"You're Linda's aunt, Mother, that's all that people have to know. They don't need to know you're the mother of his former bride-to-be."

Helen let out her breath slowly. "That's lovely of you, dear, but I'm not sure I should leave you alone with all you've been through. On the other hand, I want to be there for Linda. I don't know what to do."

"Mother, I'll be just fine, really. I feel better than I have in a long time. Besides, someone has to feed Nubbins."

That drew a smile from her mother, breaking the tension.

Helen put a hand on Carrie's shoulder. "God has a purpose in all of this. We may not be able to see what it is right now, but that doesn't mean it is all for naught. Doesn't His Word say that all things work together for good to those who love Him and are called according to His purpose? We were calling Him a miracle-working God and determining not to give up hope before we heard the news of Scott. Let's just give this situation with Linda and Andrew into His hands."

"You're right, Mother, I guess it is always easier to have faith when it doesn't touch your own family."

Helen sighed. "Linda has always gone her own way, not matter what we said or did. She had a good home with a family who loved her, yet she was always willful. I hope she hasn't gotten herself into something she can't handle."

"Linda will work this out," Carrie assured her. "Andrew is a good man in many ways. We may be surprised. Now I don't know about you, but I'm starving. What's for dinner?"

CHAPTER TWENTY-SIX

*T*HE NEXT TWO days passed slowly as the people of the valley watched and waited. The helicopters continued to dip into the river, carrying their burdens of precious water. Aerial bombers still roared past overhead to cover the mountain with their chemicals, creating huge reddish clouds. Carrie could almost hear the ticking of the clock within her that marked the days and hours as she and neighbors waited. The fire was fifty per cent contained, then seventy-five per cent contained, and as the end of the week neared, ninety per cent contained.

Carrie walked Nubbins and spent time on the bench by the river. The Spencers kept them posted on news of Scott. He had rested and accepted some medical aid, but insisted on returning to the fire lines.

Linda called again, seeking to explain and keep them posted on what was happening. Helen had even spoken to Andrew and her countenance was somewhat lifted. Carrie realized she and her mother had a lot to tell her father when he returned home.

The sky began to clear and the taint of burning that had lingered in the air began to decrease. By the end of the week the firemen were gone from their meadow and the water trucks no longer labored up their road. The red CDF trucks disappeared almost overnight.

Carrie, her family, and neighbors stood at the end of their driveways, on their porches, and on the road to view the mountains, now stripped and blackened by the fire; the reality and presence of the trauma their valley had suffered. Yet when turning away, where the mountain was hidden by the stand of pine trees at the end of the driveway, it seemed to Carrie that it was like a dream, a nightmare from which they could all awaken.

One of the rangers shared with her the story of a small seed pod that only opens under the high temperatures of a fire. There was a purpose to everything in nature. She thought of the people the fire had affected—the relationships that had been exposed to the light of the fire. A cleansing, refining fire, sweeping away the dross, and leaving only what was real.

Her relationship with Andrew had been shallow and built on transient things. Like the house built on the sand, it had crumbled when put to the ultimate test. Now, in her quiet hours, she built her own spiritual house on the Rock that was her Lord. She strengthened the timbers with His Word and laid a foundation in her soul that He could build upon. Turning herself in the direction of His choosing, she waited, at peace with God and with herself.

It was Sunday evening when the one for whom she waited came. Just after the supper dishes were done, she was contemplating a walk with Nubbins. She opened the front door and they were face to face.

She let the wonder of his presence move over her with warmth that slowly made its way to her face and mouth as she smiled at him.

"Hello, Scott."

"Hello yourself," he said softly, his eyes never leaving her face. "I'm off fire duty and thought I'd drop by…" He grinned. "Well, it's not too far, considering I'm living in your yard."

"Won't you come in?"

"Actually, I was wondering if you'd like to go for a walk?"

This time she laughed. "I was just thinking of doing that with Nubbins."

They slowly walked side by side down to the river bank and on the little path along the river.

"I've had a lot of questions since the fire started. I didn't want to pry into your life, but when Linda left with Andrew, I prayed that you were all right. There just wasn't time to talk with all of you having to leave, and then the fire to fight. Can you talk about it now?"

They came back to the bench and sat down.

"Yes, I can tell you about it, Scott. God had been trying to get through to me for some time. I just didn't want to listen. Andrew was wrong for me. I guess I was dazed by all the glitter and the prestige of marrying into so much money. I thought I truly loved Andrew, but I didn't." She hung her head. "I was handy—picked out by his father because he thought I'd make a good, pliable wife for his son." She told him about the trust and Andrew's need to marry. "I guess his grandfather was aware of Andrew's lifestyle even then. Andrew's father convinced him the business needed the money. Andrew had let time go by and now his thirtieth birthday was approaching. I guess I was a willing pawn in their grand scheme of things and I'm not very proud of the fact."

"And Linda?"

"Remember she said they met a year or so ago? He was leaving a party, a little drunk, as has been the case many times evidently. She saw him leave and realized he needed help so she put him in a cab. All he saw of her was her golden dress and face and golden hair. When he was sober the next day, he realized he didn't know her name. He just called her his 'golden angel'. She'd just come to the party briefly with a friend of a friend and no one knew who she was."

"And, they met again that afternoon you brought him home?"

"Yes. Linda and I had a scene before going to sleep. Then, in the night something woke me up. I realized Linda wasn't in her bed and went down to Andrew's room. He was gone too. I went out on the porch, feeling confused. I heard voices down here by the bench and then saw them come up the path. They were deep in conversation and I thought Linda was trying to hit on Andrew."

"How did you feel about that?" His voice was soft, gentle.

"At first, angry and betrayed, all very righteous feelings, I guess. I hurried back up to my room and waited for Linda to return and then confronted her. She told me that Andrew would marry me to please his father, if I insisted. Then, she said that if I did marry Andrew, I would ruin not only my life but others."

"Which others?"

She searched his face as she answered, for her heart hung in the balance and she didn't want to feel foolish.

"Andrew's...and yours." To her wonder and delight, she saw in his eyes what she had been hoping and praying for all week.

He reached up and brushed a leaf out of her hair, then gently cupped her chin in his hand. "Linda is a very perceptive woman. She saw what I have been trying to hide since the day you first arrived home. I think I have loved you since I was in high school, but you were such a frightened little thing every time I was around you."

She gave him a sheepish grin. "I was in awe, I guess, you were the big football star."

"Those blue eyes of yours did things to my heart. I couldn't forget you, even after I went off to college."

He rose and took her by the shoulders, lifting her against him and holding her close. It seemed so natural to slide her arms around him.

"I couldn't believe you weren't married, Scott. Every eligible girl in school threw herself at you."

"Maybe we go after the ones who don't throw themselves at us. You just looked like you needed someone to look after you."

She laughed softly again, feeling safe against him. "Maybe I do. I don't seem to make very good decisions on my own."

"The decision to let go of Andrew, for Linda's sake and your own, took courage and wisdom."

"Courage from the Lord, Scott. If I hadn't found Him, again, I would still be on the wrong path."

He bent his head down to hers. "And now, young lady, since you are no longer engaged, I'm going to press my advantage." This time his kiss was anything but brotherly.

At last, they parted slightly and he held her again. She felt the strong beating of his heart as he murmured in her ear.

"I saw your face in my mind when I thought it was the end. I wanted to have one last chance to hold you, to tell you I loved you, and beg you not to marry Andrew. When He and Linda left together, I wanted to run to you, to find out what had happened. It just wasn't possible under the circumstances. Now God has given us that chance. This time I'm not letting you go."

"Don't ever let me go, Scott. Wherever you are I want to be."

Taking her by the hand, they started up the path to share the good news with her parents, and this time Carrie knew she didn't have to worry about their reaction. As they came by the meadow, she looked up into the sky full of stars, the first clear sky in many days. A breeze swayed the trees and ruffled her hair. She sniffed the night air.

"Oh, Scott, the wind has blown the smoke away, at last."

"It's about time," he grinned, and they walked toward the house together.

LaVergne, TN USA
05 January 2010
168858LV00005B/115/P